Uncle Adolf

Craig Cormick

Uncle Adolf

This book was written with the assistance of an artsACT project grant

Uncle Adolf
ISBN 978 1 74027 864 5
Copyright © text Craig Cormick 2014

First published 2014
Reprinted 2016

GINNINDERRA PRESS

PO Box 3461 Port Adelaide 5015
www.ginninderrapress.com.au

'The great masses of the people will more easily
fall victim to a big lie than a small one.'
— *Mein Kampf*

Eins

From millions of men…one man must step forward who with apodictic
force will form granite principles from the wavering idea-world of the
broad masses and take up the struggle for their sole correctness…

– Mein Kampf

The old bus wheezes a bit on the hills and, as it slows for another climb, the foreigner looks out the window and examines the wasteland of another logged-out forest. It brings to mind distant memories of the aftermath of battles he has seen. It is a dislocating feeling and he turns back to look at the passenger seated beside him. As soon as he does, he knows it is a mistake. He's getting better at recognising them in his old age.

As if waiting for the chance to re-engage him, the old digger asks him, once again, 'So, Hungarian, was it you said?'

The foreigner tries hard not to roll his eyes. 'Yes, that's right. Hungarian,' he says, then he turns back to the window.

The battle memory is gone and they are now cruising down a slope, passing through thick scrub on either side of the bus. The foreigner wishes he could see the ocean. He also wishes he'd gone to the toilet in Narooma. They'd only stopped once since then, to let a dozen men climb off and piss on the bus's tyres.

'You were on our side then, weren't you?' the old digger asks him.

The foreigner twists a little in his seat. They are vinyl and have seen better days, like most of the passengers, and are uncomfortable to sit on for so long a journey.

'Your side of the bus?' asks the foreigner.

'No. Our side in the war,' says the old digger.

'Yes. We fought the Germans, then the Russians.'

The old digger mulls on that a moment. 'Fair enough,' he says, then points at the large curved scar on the foreigner's forehead. 'That where you got that?'

The foreigner nods once, having abandoned the banal truth of the street brawl with fellow thugs years ago. 'Of course,' he says. 'A very serious head wound.'

The digger then nods in turn and says, 'Did I mention that I was at Tobruk?'

'I think you did,' says the foreigner, trying to look busy, studying the form guide from the previous day's paper in his hands. He has found an unexpected pleasure in betting on horses, and has also found that for a man so obsessed with details it is less a gamble than a calculation, and could be quite profitable. At times.

'Yairs,' says the old digger. 'We taught those Nazi scum a thing or two. Showed 'em what Australian troops are really worth.' He points at the newspaper, 'Like the Brits are going to show those Argies a thing or two.'

The foreigner doesn't need to look to know he is pointing at the large black headlines proclaiming the latest British propaganda about the war in the Falklands. He's written enough propaganda in his years to know well-crafted lies, regardless of the size of the type they are in.

The digger takes a deep breath, like he is about to go off on another track of thought, but is quiet for a moment and the foreigner hopes he's gone back to sleep. The sight of the man's dentures dropping half out of his mouth appals him, but it is preferable to his constant interrogation about the war.

But the old digger turns back suddenly and says, 'Do you know what Rommel called us?'

'Yes,' says the foreigner. 'The forty-thousand thieves!'

'That's right,' says the old digger. 'But we showed him. Didn't we.'

'Yes,' he replies, looking at his watch, wishing the journey was over already.

He looks out the window again. A dark brown panel van, with two surfboards on its roof racks and the word SANDMAN on the sides, overtakes the bus, its V8 engine roaring loudly.

Presently the bus passes a road sign and the foreigner sees they're only ten miles from his destination. He feels his heart beating a little harder. It's just the excitement, he tells himself. He sits there and counts off the miles. Once an impatient man, he's become very good at waiting. Every now and then he can glimpse the ocean through the trees. It won't be long now, he tells himself. Twenty years waiting for this!

'How did you know that?' asks the old digger suddenly. 'About us being the forty-thousand thieves?'

'Um – I think somebody told me,' says the foreigner.

'Was it somebody who fought in the war?' asks the old digger.

'Yes, I'm certain it was,' he says.

'What was his name?' asks the old digger. 'Maybe I knew him.'

'His name was Erwin Rommel,' says the foreigner and smirks a little.

But the old digger doesn't see anything funny in it. 'A lot of good people died at Tobruk,' he says truculently. Then, 'You sure the Hungarians were on our side?'

But all the foreigner says is, 'Yes, a lot of good people died there.'

That appeases the old digger somewhat and he lapses into silence for some time. When the foreigner looks back, he's dozing and his dentures have fallen half out of his mouth. The foreigner shakes his head and wonders, not for the first time, how they had managed to hold Tobruk for so long.

He settles back in his seat and tries to find a more comfortable position. His back hurts and he feels a pressing urgency on his bladder. The curses of old age. But they're small discomforts today, and the journey will soon be over.

Twenty years, he ponders again.

The bus speaker system crackles overhead and the driver says, 'Eden, five minutes.'

His travel companion startles awake. 'What did he say?' he asks.

'Eden,' he tells him.

'Oh,' says the old digger. 'I've a way to go yet.'

'Well, it's my stop,' the foreigner says. 'So if you'll excuse me.'

'Sure,' says the old digger and rises slowly from his seat to let him squeeze past him.

'Thank you,' the foreigner mumbles.

'It's Len,' the old digger suddenly says, with the stranger pressed up close against him. 'Len Wicks.' And he holds out his hand.

The foreigner stares at it as if the man has offered him his dentures to hold, but he takes it and says, after a pause, 'Joseph Lukas.' The name is well worn in his mouth, but never comes as quickly as he'd like it to.

'It's gonna be a holiday, is it?' Len asks him.

'No. I'm visiting an old comrade.'

'Ah,' says Len wistfully. 'I know the feeling of that.'

'I'm sure,' says the foreigner and he squeezes past Len Wicks, falling against him just for a moment as the bus lurches.

Both men look a little awkward and it breaks the need for any further conversations.

The foreigner makes his way down to the front of the bus as they round the last few curves in the road and suddenly the sea fills up the whole vista in front of them. Blue and sparkling. He stares at it for some moments and then nearly topples over as the bus comes to a stop.

The driver opens the door with a pneumatic hiss, and then helps him find his bag.

The foreigner stands there by the roadside until the bus is gone in a cloud of exhaust and the grinding of gears. Then he reaches into his pocket and looks through Len Wicks's wallet. A few cards and photos and not much cash. A poor travelling companion in every sense, he thinks.

Then he turns his back to the ocean and starts walking up the small hill to his right. He pulls out a piece of paper to check on the directions he has been given. He is panting after five minutes, but keeps on. Only a little further, he tells himself. The ache in his back. The need to urinate. The wheezing in his breath. They are nothing. This is a momentous day. And then he can see the house. A two-storey building looming over the road before him.

He stands there a moment, his lips gone suddenly dry. He has imagined this for so long. Imagined just how it would feel to be standing here. But the brick veneer building with a flat roof and veranda mounted on white metal poles is very different to what he had pictured in his mind. He had been imagining something more – well, Bavarian.

But then he sees the glass door to the second-storey veranda slide open. And a dog steps out onto the veranda. A German shepherd. It looks down at him. Then a man steps out behind it and stands there. Also looking down at him. Hands clasped behind his back.

The foreigner blinks. It is him. Now it is just how he had pictured it. And twenty years means nothing. He has to contain himself not to drop his bag to the road and shout out, '*Sieg Heil*.'

He might have too, but at that moment a young boy, about ten or eleven years old, steps out on the veranda and takes the Führer's hand. 'Hello,' he says shyly. 'You must be Uncle Martin!'

Uncle's new friend has a large red nose like he was been bitten by a bee. *Apis* in Latin. There are over 20,000 species of bees. He is taller than Uncle. I would like to ask him how tall. Uncle is 173 centimetres, if you include the curve of his back, which he says I must. That is five feet and eight inches. He said he was taller before he got old. Much, much, much taller.

He says I can call him Uncle even though he's not my real uncle. I have two real uncles. One is named Robert, but he prefers to be called Bob. He is my mother's brother. He is two years and twenty-three days older than her. He lives in Sydney and works as a truck driver. He comes to visit us every Christmas and stays for one week. He says he will take me for a drive in his truck one day. He doesn't drive a truck when he comes to visit us, though. He drives a Ford Falcon 500XY. He says it is just the same age as me, which is nine years and fifty-one days, and that it is the best car ever made.

It is 198 days until next Christmas.

Uncle's new friend says I should call him Joseph, but Uncle has already told me that his real name is Martin. I asked if he drove trucks, but Uncle said, 'No. He does not drive trucks.' I asked if he would stay for one week. Uncle said perhaps.

I don't like perhapses.

My other uncle is Bruno. He is the brother of my father and he only came to visit when I was very small. When my father still lived with us. And he has been gone for five years and forty-seven days. My mother says he has gone to buggery. I asked if that is near Sydney, but she only laughed. She says that Uncle Bruno is in Sydney, though. He lives at a place called Long Bay and Mother says he won't visit anybody for Christmas for at least another ten years. I asked if he will come and visit us then. She said another perhaps.

Our town is also on a Bay. Twofold Bay. Sydney is 373 kilometres away. Which is closer in miles – 231 miles only. Uncle says that Uncle Martin has been in Sydney though he does not live there. He lives at a place called anonymously.

My mother says that Uncle is a kind man to look after me when she is feeling under the weather. She stays in bed many mornings because she is often under the weather. She says I can go and play with Uncle but that I should not annoy him or he will send me back home. He has never sent me back home, though. Uncle says he enjoys the company of a quiet boy, but I am allowed to ask him questions. He says many things are our secrets. Like Mummy says it is a secret that Uncle Bruno lives at Long Bay. It is a secret that Uncle's friend is really named Martin. It is not a secret that my Uncle Bob's really name is Robert, though.

Uncle's friend has another name too. Uncle calls him *kamerad*. I would like a secret name. Uncle calls me Adam. Mummy calls me Pumpkin. Uncle's friend calls me Boy. 'Hello, boy,' he says.

Uncle says that I should like him. But he also says to keep my eyes on my loose change when his friend is around. He smiles so I know that this is a joke. Jokes can be very difficult to understand. Mummy says not to lose any sleep over jokes. She says that they are not as funny as most people think they are. She says life is less funny as you get older. I don't think life is very funny at nine years and fifty-one days.

Mummy also says that life is a bitch. A bitch is a female dog. We don't have a dog. Uncle has a dog called Blondi. She doesn't have any other names. But she is an Alsatian, which is also called a German shepherd. It doesn't have a Latin name because the breed is newer than Latin, which is an old language. But dog in Latin is *Canis lupus familiaris*.

Uncle says that Blondi is about the same age as me. I ask him how many years and days exactly she is, but he says he doesn't know exactly. He says that in dog years Blondi is almost as old as him. He says a dog year is worth seven of our years. In dog years, I would be turning eighty in one week, and Uncle would be 651.

I told him this and he said, 'Perhaps.'

Zwei

Mankind has grown strong in eternal struggle, and
only in eternal peace does it perish.

– Mein Kampf

Martin Bormann watches Hitler carry out a small silver tray, heaped high with an army of tiny cream cakes. The Führer's hands still tremble, he sees, but it does not appear as bad as when he had last seen him. He is more stooped, though. His hair is whiter and thinner and his face is that of a very old man. He would ponder his own appearance more and how the burden of his life has left its mark on him, but his most pressing thoughts are actually to use the Führer's toilet. He hopes this will not be a cause of problems as he remembers well how nobody was ever allowed to use his toilet in the Bunker or the Wolf's Lair. Not even Eva. Poor Eva. He will ask about her one day.

The Führer is already sitting, next to the young boy, stuffing a cake with little angel wings into his mouth, when Bormann, says, 'I must use your facilities. It is rather urgent.'

Hitler looks at him blankly a moment, as if he might be referring to a radio room or some such, but then he sees the urgency in Bormann's eyes and understands. 'You can use the guest facilities,' he says. 'They are downstairs.' Hitler passes a cake to the boy.

Bormann thanks him and makes his way down the stairs that Hitler indicates. The house, he sees, is made of large concrete blocks, with wooden panelling covering it. The downstairs is, like many houses on the south coast, sparse and designed for storage. There is a familiar smell of concrete dust and damp about the place that makes Bormann recall the bunker under the Reich Chancellery. There is a small metal-framed bunk bed in one corner of the room he descends into, and the toilet is behind a small door that is a little warped and needs to be forced open.

It is apparent that the Führer has not had guests for many years. The water has evaporated out of the bowel and the seat is covered in dust. Martin Bormann stands there and pisses the feeble and frustrating piss of an old man. Then he makes his way back upstairs.

'Did you wash your hands?' the Führer demands of him in English.

'Yes,' Bormann lies.

'Good. Then have a cream cake.' The Führer picks one cake from the large dish in front of him, places it on a small plate and passes it to Bormann.

The German shepherd dog limps up beside him as he sits at the small table by the Führer and emits one of those ghastly and silent dog farts that only old dogs can produce. The boy giggles, as only boys can giggle when somebody farts. Bormann coughs and looks down at the dog accusingly.

'Blondi is getting old,' the Führer says, 'but still has a keen sense of duty to protect me from menace.'

Bormann doubts that the dog's gas attacks would actually prove lethal, and seeing the dog up close he suspects this might be its most fearsome attribute. 'How old is she?' he asks politely.

'I stopped counting at ten,' the Führer says. 'I find it is a good philosophy for life.'

'I'm sure she still has a lot of life in her yet,' says Bormann.

'As do we all,' Hitler says, holding him with those piercing eyes of his. Still hypnotically intense in his ninth decade.

Bormann bites into his cream cake and watches the Führer eat a second and then a third.

Finally, after his eleventh cake, or perhaps twelfth, for Bormann has stopped counting at ten, he sits back in his chair, satisfied, and says, 'It has been a long time.'

'Twenty years,' says Bormann.

'Twenty-one, I believe,' says Hitler. 'I'm sure the last time we met was at the home of that Ustashe in 1961.'

Bormann squints as if looking into the past. The Führer is right, as ever. It was in 1961. They had met up on a farm south of Sydney, owned by a former Croatian SS officer. They had not seen each other since they had been released from Bonegilla refugee camp.

'You were going to have plastic surgery to remove that scar over your right eye,' Hitler says.

'Yes,' shrugs Bormann. 'It seemed less important with every passing year.' He would add that nobody even knows the name of Martin Bormann these days, let alone might still be searching for him, but he is a little unsure of what to say in the boy's presence. He is surprised to see that Hitler has regrown his moustache, though, and is combing his thinning white hair in his old style once more. It would be foolish to think that anybody would ever forget the name of Adolf Hitler.

Suddenly a cuckoo clock on the wall erupts into singing and the Führer turns his head and says, 'It is time for some urgently needed news!'

Bormann, still a little disoriented, blinks rapidly. He had been planning to wait a day or two before telling the Führer, and he hesitates a moment, looking across at the boy again. But Hitler is out of his chair and making his way to the television.

Then Bormann understands. The Führer had meant news of the war! He stands and follows Hitler who is now wrestling with the reception of an old black and white television set. The picture is distorted but the sound is fine. The newsreader is talking about the progress of the British invasion force, and saying that the British government has released details of the latest casualties. Two British ships, *Sir Galahad* and *Sir Tristam*, were bombed while preparing to disembark troops, with a death toll of over fifty, and a landing craft carrying vehicles was also sunk. However, in return the British shot down three Argentinian Skyhawk planes.

Hitler stands in front of the television transfixed until the next story starts up, about an Australian athlete breaking the world record for gumboot throwing, then as if he has suddenly snapped out of a trance, he proclaims, 'Splendid! Splendid!' Then he turns to Bormann and says, 'They are grand strategists, the Argentinians. Perhaps one of our generals is advising them?'

'Perhaps,' says Bormann doubtfully.

'Mengele has assured me he has the full confidence of the Argentinian military,' Hitler says.

'Of course,' says Bormann, glancing across at the boy again, who is smiling back at them both. Perhaps he is a simpleton, Bormann thinks, so the Führer can talk openly in front of him.

'Did you visit him on your last trip to Argentina?' Hitler asks.

'Uh – no – it was not possible to see him,' Bormann says in German.

'It's a pity,' says the Führer, in English. 'But he was undoubtedly preoccupied with preparations for this war.' Then he suddenly grows a little pensive. 'It will be a pity to see Mrs Thatcher defeated. She is an admirable woman in many ways.'

And Bormann has a sudden unbidden image of Mrs Thatcher in Germanic opera costume, as one of the Valkyries, with a low-cut metal and leather bustier and her hair in plaits. He finds it quite enticing.

'Come,' says the Führer. 'I will show you something.' And he leads Bormann across to the large wooden table in the dining area. The Führer sits down and begins sorting through the array of papers there.

Bormann sees that many are clippings from tabloid newspapers. And there are sketches and maps. All of the Falklands war.

The Führer digs out a large sketch of the Falkland Islands he has made, that has red and blue pencil lines all over it, showing the progress of the war. 'Come closer,' the Führer says and Bormann leans in closer. Just like in the old days in the bunker. 'Not you,' the Führer says, and Bormann sees that Hitler had meant the young boy.

He sucks in his cheeks and frowns.

Hitler points at the map with a trembling finger and asks the boy, 'Where is Port Stanley?'

'Here,' the boy says and points at it.

'Good boy,' Hitler says, and pats his cheek.

Then he turns to Bormann, who finds a glow of jealousy being fanned inside his stomach. The Führer had never patted his cheek like that!

'This is where the British believe the key to the war is, and where they are currently advancing towards,' the Führer says.

Bormann nods. He has been following the war in the newspapers too and is aware that the British forces have been wearing the Argentinians down and are poised for their final assault on Port Stanley.

'It is all a clever stratagem,' the Führer says. 'Like my invasion of France. Make the enemy think you are somewhere and then surprise them from the rear!'

Bormann squints at the map then takes his glasses out of his pocket and looks at it closely. 'So where are the Argentinian forces?' he asks, for he cannot see where else they might possibly be except at Port Stanley.

'It does not matter where they are,' says the Führer. 'It is more important to understand that they are not where the British think they are. It is all a clever ruse. A bluff. They have a surprise stratagem in hand.' And he begins pounding one fist upon his palm and going a deep red in the face. 'Don't you see it?'

'Of course, *mein Führer*,' says Bormann. 'But it has taken your brilliance to point it out to me.'

The Führer calms a little and says, 'Yes. Not everybody is blessed with a natural military mind.' Then he sorts through the press clippings and maps and says, 'Do you know, Bormann, that while the British were our enemy, I always had hopes they would join with us. We have much in common, you know. We should have formed an alliance against the *Untermenschen*.'

Bormann has heard this all before, many years ago in the bunker. Hitler's belief that when the Allied and Russian forces met, the Allies would see the need to form an alliance with Germany to beat back the

Bolshevik forces. And he has heard Hitler espousing how the Cold War should have been avoided by crushing Russia in the 1940s. He looks again to the young boy for his reaction. But he is busy tracing imaginary battle lines on the map with his finger. Bormann longs to know what the boy is thinking.

'If we'd had leaders like Mrs Thatcher and Mr Reagan during our war, things would have turned out very different, you know,' he tells Martin Bormann.

'I have no doubt of it,' says Bormann.

'But the Argentinians are our allies now,' he says. Then, 'And you assure me there is much German blood in the race?'

'*Ja, mein Führer,*' says Bormann. 'The Argentinians have much German and Italian blood as well as Spanish. All good fascist races.'

Hitler nods. 'I envy you your travels,' he tells Bormann. 'It would be a wonderful thing to keep in personal contact with our colleagues as you do.'

Bormann, for his part, quite envies the Führer his coastal sanctuary near the end of the world here. He can sit on his balcony and look out over the vast blue Pacific Ocean every day, and can live in the past or the present or the future, or whatever era he wishes. It will be a pity to tell him the news, he thinks.

And suddenly he sees the Führer's eyes bulge a little. He sees him purse his lips tightly.

'Oh dear,' he says.

Bormann hears a creaking that at first he presumes is the pipes in the house but then understands is the Führer's insides. 'Too many cream cakes?' he asks.

'Nonsense,' says the Führer. 'Just the trials of old age.' And he rises to his feet and shuffles quickly down the small hallway to his private toilet.

The young boy remains at the table, tracing imaginary lines on the map of the Falkland Islands. And Bormann finds that he envies him anew. How wonderful to live in an imaginary world, he thinks.

Uncle's new friend has funny eyes. They keep looking at me until I look back at him. Then they are suddenly looking somewhere else. Like it is a game he is playing with me. My favourite game is Uno. That is a card game. You put down cards that match colours and numbers. If you keep a count of what cards have already been put down, it is easy to know what cards are left. Mummy sometimes plays Uno with me. She says I'm a natural. She says I'm a card shark. I tell her I'm a card dolphin. I don't like sharks.

Uncle says mothers are always right. I ask him about his mother. Her name was Klara. My mother's name is Eve. Uncle says once had a very special friend called Eva – which is almost the same. He says he misses her. He also says that it was probably a joke of my father to name me Adam. It's not a very funny joke.

Uncle says his name is also very similar to mine. Our birthdays are only one day apart too. But his father's name was Alois and my father's name was Rick. He says that his father left him too. He doesn't say anything else about his father, except that it is okay to be angry at your father for leaving you with nothing but a name.

Sometimes Uncle gets sad like my mother does, but he doesn't get under the weather. When he is sad, he gets out his maps and teaches me how to read them. They are all about colours and numbers too. They can be almost as much fun as Uno. Uno is Latin for one. You say it when you have only one card left in your hand. Uncle says you should always hold more than one card in your hand when you are at the end of the game. I tell him that he doesn't understand Uno's rules. But he says he is not bound by rules, and I tell him that I won't be able to play Uno with him if he doesn't follow the rules. I tell him that Mummy always follows the rules and he laughs and tells me that she is a very good mother then. But she doesn't play Uno with me as often as I would like her to.

I wonder if Uncle's friend knows how to play it? Though, if he does, I will have to be careful and make sure that he doesn't have more than one card in his hand when he says Uno.

Martin Bormann is walking up the steps to the Führer's Wolf's Lair again. This time he has saluted his leader from the street. Has proudly thrust his arm up at a straight angle and clicked his boots together.

The Führer is much younger this time. His hair is still dark, and the stoop to his back is less pronounced. Like he was the last time Bormann had seen him. And Bormann himself is younger too. His legs do not ache and his fingers are strong when he clenches them. It is a glorious feeling. His Führer beckons him to come to him, with arms spread wide and Bormann, for a moment, wants to run across a field of spring flowers towards his leader's embrace – but then he is on the stairs leading up the balcony. The balcony of the Eagle's Lair in Bavaria. It is a wide concrete construction that looks out over the valley.

He takes the next few stairs easily enough, but then his feet feel heavy and he looks down. His jackboots have been replaced by old leather shoes that pinch his feet, and there is a sudden tiredness in his legs. No matter, he thinks. He will not be slowed by such minor irritations on this day, and he keeps climbing. But each step is taller than the one before it. Each more effort to climb. He looks up and sees his Führer is further away than he had been a moment before. He is atop a large tower that he must ascend to rescue him. He presses his hands onto the tops of his thighs for extra leverage and pushes, feeling his aged limbs click and creak in protest.

Suddenly he is short of breath. He wants to sit down and rest, but knows that if he stops he will never be able to continue. He must keep going. And Hitler is calling to him, urging him to keep on going. Bormann feels an ache in his back as he takes one more step. Then another.

He is wearing old slippers now, he sees, and his hands are gnarled and his fingers swollen. His legs are sore and wobbling under his weight. But he must keep going. He must.

Then metal spikes and barbed wire start growing across the steps to tangle him up. He tears his slippers, but won't be deterred. He curses and grits his teeth.

Next he sees his way is blocked by a descending stream of wounded German soldiers, limping and stumbling down the stairs. He shoulders them aside, until one of his feet becomes entangled in the barbed wire. He pulls at it and the foot suddenly comes off. He looks down at it in amazement. He grabs a crutch from a wounded soldier and continues climbing the stairs. He looks up to see where his Führer is, but he can no longer see him. He can hear him, though, calling out to him, urging him on.

Then suddenly it is dark on the steps and he can see furtive shapes in dark coats all around him. Black-gloved hands reach for him. He swings the crutch at them like a sword, clearing a path ahead of him. He takes several more large steps until he is free of them. But he is so tired. If he could just sit down for a moment, he could regain his energy, he thinks. If he could just sit in the little darkened room in the flat in the small South American town, no one would ever find him. It is just ahead of him. Inviting him in to rest.

But again he hears his Führer's voice, calling him to come to him. He wants to sit and cry. To call out that he cannot go on, but now he is in an empty place. Utterly alone. He looks back and the stairs behind him have crumbled away to nothing. He must keep climbing or the steps will crumble beneath his feet. His foot! He will plummet into the dark nothingness. And that fills him with a dread beyond any of the many fears that have filled his life. Urging him on. The barbed wire means nothing. The height of the steps is nothing. The pain in his aged body is nothing. If he does not reach the top of the steps and fall into his Führer's waiting embrace, he will cease to exist. Will be erased from being. Will be gone from history.

He wants to call out to his Führer to ask him to help him, to reach out an arm to him, but no words come out. He takes another step. Then another. And suddenly the path is easier. He is walking on level ground. There is a train track here at the top of the stairs, running into the darkness. But there are Russian voices all around. And gunfire and explosions make him wince.

'Come,' says the Führer, who is suddenly in front of him, holding out his hand to him. 'This way.'

But Bormann is afraid to move. He wants to tunnel into the stones and dirt and hide there.

'Come,' says the Führer once more.

Bormann is crying now. Afraid to take another step. Then the shells start falling around them. The ground between him and the Führer is being torn apart by shell fire.

'Come,' says the Führer more insistently, and then turns and walks into the darkness.

And Bormann feels the terrible dread of that night upon him. That dread of ceasing to be. The worse fear he has ever known. A fear worse than dying. But it is a fear that saves him, as he runs from it into the darkness after his Führer.

Drei

The Aryan...it was he who laid the foundations and erected
the walls of every great structure in human culture.

– Mein Kampf

Bormann wakes up with a start. His first reaction is that he has to escape. Has to drop to his hands and knees and crawl away from the fighting. It takes him a moment to realise he has fallen asleep on the couch. The Führer had been telling him about the weather patterns on the coast or something and he had dozed off on him. The Führer will be furious. Then the sound of two men shouting registers in his mind.

He sees the boy sitting passively on the other couch, just staring at him with a stupid smile on his face. Definitely something odd about that boy, he thinks. He struggles to his feet and moves cautiously towards the front door. The Führer is standing there, shouting at a man, waving a slip of paper in the air, much in way that Prime Minister Chamberlain had when he'd come back from Munich in 1938. Bormann tries to hear what the two men are arguing about so heatedly, but suddenly the Führer takes a step back and slams the door in the other man's face.

'*Was ist los?*' Bormann asks, but the Führer is beyond answering him. He stomps about the room, barely able to get the words out, spitting and grinding his teeth. Blondi slinks under the table and put her paws over her ears. Bormann isn't sure what to do as he sees veins bulging dangerously on the Führer's face. He has gone from red to purple.

'*Mein Führer?*' Bormann says, but Hitler cannot even answer him. His whole body suddenly seizes up in a shaking apoplexy and he falls to the ground. Bormann is horrified! What if he has a heart attack? What if he has a stroke? He drops to his knees by his leader and gently places his hands on his body. He feels it trembling under his touch. He tries to roll the Führer over, but he cannot. Then he sees that he has the rug firmly in his teeth, biting down on it as foam and spittle trickles out of his mouth.

'Ah,' says Bormann, relieved. He has seen this many times and knows now it is just one of the Führer's fits. He will calm down in a moment. He remembers how Eva Braun once told him, in strictest confidence, that he had no knowledge of his fits afterwards and used to blame Blondi for chewing on the rugs in the bunker. Poor Eva, he thinks. Truly an innocent amongst wolves.

He sits down on the couch again, and sees that boy just watching with that stupid smile. The Führer was always surrounded by idiots, he thinks. Together they watch Hitler roll and writhe on the floor and Bormann thinks of the terrible burdens of greatness. He had read somewhere, though he can't remember where, that Alexander the Great and Julius Caesar also had fits like this, though perhaps not triggered by rage as the Führer's were.

He sees Blondi under the table and says, 'Come here, girl.'

She slinks over to him and sits by his feet. He wonders how many dogs with this name the Führer has had since the war. The original Blondi was poisoned in the bunker in the last days. Just like Eva. He leans down to pat her but smells another one of her toxic farts and sits back in the chair again. He shakes his head. The torments of old age affect dogs as much as men, he muses, and then feels the need to urinate once more.

He wonders if the Führer will know if he uses his private toilet upstairs? He looks at the boy again and wonders if he would tell.

About twenty minutes later, Hitler is sitting on the couch which Bormann has helped him to, blinking about himself. 'I must have dozed off for a moment,' he says.

Bormann nods in an understanding way. Hitler looks down at the slip of paper in his hands and his face starts to redden a little again.

'You had a fight with a man at the door,' says Bormann. 'Something about that letter in your hand.'

'The petty tyrants of the local council,' says Hitler. 'We have been engaged in hostilities for over five years. They claim that I have invaded my neighbour's property.'

'How do you mean?' asks Bormann.

'Come, I will show you,' says Hitler, and leads him across to the dining table, where he pushes the Falklands papers asides and drags out from underneath them a large map.

Bormann looks at if for some moments and then recognises it as a shire divisional map that shows properties and drains and so on.

'Look carefully here,' says Hitler. 'This is my land.' And he stabs his finger to the map.

Bormann looks at it carefully.

'And this,' the Führer says, 'Is my neighbour's land. He is a Pole! A Slav. An *Untermensch*!'

Bormann nods.

'Now this is the area of disagreement,' says Hitler, stabbing his finger at the back corner of the two properties. 'The petty dictators of the council claim that my back shed overlaps the Slav's property by…' and he opens the letter in his hand and reads it over. '…by twenty-nine inches! And unless I withdraw my shed from his land, they will take action!'

'What type of action?' asks Bormann.

And Hitler laughs. 'What kind of action can they possibly take? Send in tanks and bombers? I don't think so.'

Bormann looks at the lines that the Führer has drawn all over the plans. It is a complicated battle plan, showing where the council will try and enter his property and the defensive lines he will use to defend his land. 'You will be fighting a defensive battle?' he asks.

And Hitler looks over the top of his glasses at him. 'Defensive battles always lose. Think of Stalingrad! If General Paulus had gone on the offensive like I repeatedly ordered him to, do you think the Russians would have recaptured the city? Certainly not. When a defensive position is called for, my strategy has always been to attack. You should know that!'

'But are you drawing a little too much attention to yourself through this? Isn't it easier to have the shed moved a small distance?' suggests Bormann cautiously.

'This is a matter of *lebensraum*!' states Hitler. 'Living space for the German people.'

Bormann frowns, unsure how the Nazi doctrine of German living space for Germans, which was used to justify the invasion of Czechoslovakia and Poland, quite applies here. 'But for 29 inches?'

And the Führer stares at his one-time secretary and looks sadly disappointed in him. 'Retreat?' he asks. 'Are you saying that I should give in to these peasants?'

And Martin Bormann licks his lips a little, decidedly uncomfortable. 'Well, no. Of course not. I'm just suggesting a more strategic approach perhaps…'

'More strategic?' Hitler asks in a thin cold voice. 'Are you saying that you might have a better sense of strategy than I? One of the greatest military minds of all time. Are you saying that you understand the situation here? Are you saying that you know better what to do than your Führer?'

He starts going red in the face again and Martin Bormann, puts on his sweetest face, as he long ago learned and says in shock horror, 'My Führer misunderstands me! I have the greatest admiration for his sense of strategy and I am only trying to perform my unending duty of trying to learn more from my Führer so that I might better myself. If I have caused any inadvertent offence, I will immediately take out my pistol and shoot myself here at your feet!' It is the same old line he used to use in the bunker when he inadvertently set the Führer off. Although back then, he really did have a pistol, though he made sure it was never loaded, just in case.

The Führer looks away and then looks back at Martin Bormann and rolls his head a little petulantly. 'So,' he says, and turns back to the map. 'The council are now stating that they are going to discuss the issue at their next council meeting with a mind to resolving it by action.'

Bormann nods slowly yet again. He wants to ask what kind of action they have at their disposal, but does not want to set Hitler off again. He wonders if they sent workmen around to forcibly dismantle his shed whether the Führer might fire on them. He supposes he still has a few guns hidden around the house as he always had. It would not be wise, he thinks. There would be police and then newspaper men and perhaps even television and then many people would start asking awkward questions. The Führer must be advised against that.

But he says, 'I know you will defeat them.'

'They are fools!' says Hitler. 'It will be like the Polish cavalry riding out against our tanks! I will crush them!' And he smacks his fist against his palm.

'I'm just thinking about Adolf Eichmann...' says Bormann.

And the Führer freezes. His eyes are suddenly like those of a rabbit in a spotlight. He looks at Martin Bormann and licks his lips. 'What do you mean?' he demands in a suddenly weak voice.

'Well,' says Bormann gently, 'the only reason the Israeli agents were able to capture him and take him to Israel is that they found him. He was not hiding well enough.'

The Führer thinks on this carefully.

'It's a matter of staying below the radar,' Bormann says. 'Of not letting yourself be found.'

Hitler stands up and goes to the window. He stares out over the Pacific Ocean for some time. Then he comes back and sits down again.

Bormann knows he has touched the right nerve. They all have nightmares about being kidnapped from their homes like Eichmann. Of having a man come up to them in the street one day to ask for directions, or to ask for the nearest bus stop or something, and then before you knew it you were in the back of a van with a half a dozen Israeli agents, binding your mouth and pumping you full of drugs. Then you were whisked across the oceans and were suddenly on display to the world's press in a small glass cage in a Jewish court room.

'I think your advice is not well thought out,' says Hitler. 'I don't think I should engage the enemy in direct confrontation at this point. Being a master strategist means knowing when to strike and when to wait.'

'Of course,' says Bormann. 'I bow to my Führer's wisdom in this.'

'Fine,' says Hitler, and nods once, then twice. 'It is settled. We shall not engage in open warfare with the peasants on the council just yet.'

'I understand,' says Bormann.

'No. Not just yet,' Hitler muses. Then he stands and walks back to the front room. He smiles at the idiot boy and rubs his head.

Then Bormann sees him pause and look down at the rug. He rubs his foot over one patch and then shakes his head. 'Do you know,' he says. 'Blondi has a terrible habit of chewing the rug. But I can never catch her at it.' He shakes his head with that same disappointed look he had used on Bormann.

Uncle's cuckoo clock on the lounge room wall says cuckoo five times. That means it is five o'clock and time to go home. Mummy said I should come home at five o'clock today. If she doesn't give me a time to come home by, I can stay until Uncle asks me what time I should be at home, and if I say that Mummy did not give me a time to be home, he sometimes says I can stay just a little longer, although sometimes he says that perhaps it is time I went home. Another perhaps.

I say goodbye politely to Uncle and his friend using the *Auf Wiedersehen* expression. It is another name for goodbye. A secret name. I think it is good that Uncle's friend has come to visit him now because he can help him when he falls down on the floor. I can't pick Uncle up and have to just sit beside him, counting his breathing until he wakes up again.

I walk down the street to our house. It is seven houses and 269 steps away. That is a prime number, which means it can't be divided by any other number, so it is a strong number. Some days our house is a little further away, or a little closer, but as I get near to home I am counting carefully so I know if I need to take bigger or smaller steps to make it come out at just 269 steps. I worry that one day I will be taking steps that are all too small and when I reach step 268 I will be too far from home and I could not even reach it with a big jump. I would have to stand there all day and night until somebody came along to help me. Perhaps Uncle's friend could pick me up and help me take a very large step by carrying me, so it would all work out okay.

Mummy says I'm silly about numbers sometimes, but I tell her I'm a dolphin, not a shark, because dolphins know there is safety in numbers. I don't actually know if dolphins can count and do maths, but I imagine they can. They are the next most intelligent animal after humans, though Mummy says she knows plenty of humans who are more stupid than a dolphin.

I get home in exactly 269 steps and go in the front door. I look around and find Mummy in the lounge room. She has fallen down on the floor too. I know she will wake up eventually, though. I stand by her and listen to her breathing for a while. I like it when she comes into my bedroom and lies down beside me and I can hear her breathing. I count 269 breaths and then I go into the kitchen to make us dinner. Sandwiches tonight.

I lay out all the ingredients. Bread. Butter. Jam. Vegemite. And one knife for each jar. I lay them out in a special pattern. I sometimes draw a map of how I lay them out, the way Uncle has taught me to make maps. I put two slices of bread in the middle and surround it by the butter on one side and the jam and Vegemite on the other. Then I lay out the knives between them, pointing the way that the spreads are going to attack the bread.

The bread is a castle and the spreads must assail it. The butter must always go first, but I take the lid off the jam first. That is called a feint.

Then I quickly take the butter and spread it on to the bread. That is the initial thrust. Now I have to get the jam onto one piece of bread and the Vegemite onto the other. This a dual thrust. I always put the jam on first. Then I place another piece of bread on top of each. That is the sealing move. And finally I take a clean knife from the drawer and cut the bread into four long thin pieces. When they are toasted, they are called soldiers, but when they are sandwiches they are just slices.

I eat my two sandwiches and then make two more for Mummy. This time putting the Vegemite on before the jam. She is still not awake. I pick up the empty bottle from the floor and wipe up where it has spilled, and then lie down beside her.

I count her breaths waiting for her to awaken. 269, and then 269 more and then 269 more.

Vier

Armies for the preservation of peace do not exist: they
exist only for the triumphant exertion of war.

– *Mein Kampf*

The two old men eat their meal in front of the television, watching a lengthy news report on the Falklands war. Hitler has dug out of the fridge a pre-prepared meal of mashed carrots and pumpkin and potatoes. He tells Bormann that one of the local churches delivers them to him as a part of its Meals on Wheels service. There is a sprightly little Austrian lady who brings them once a week and likes to practise her German with him, he says.

Bormann has readied himself for the high-fibre vegetarian meals he knows the Führer will serve up, by having subsisted solely on meat pies during his trip down the coast. To his mind, it is not natural that a man does not eat meat. He has read, somewhere, though he can't remember where, that it was the protein in meat that enabled man's brain to grow to the size it is. That it was meat that enabled the master race to evolve above others. But he keeps that to himself.

Even Blondi gets a dish of the mashed vegetables to eat. He has to admit, however, that it is much easier on his aged gums and false teeth than the gristly meat pies were.

'This will keep you regular,' says Hitler. 'It is very important that a man pass a healthy stool every day at a regular time. I myself defecate each morning exactly at nine a.m. What about you, Bormann? How are your stools?'

Bormann lowers his fork and tries not to wince. He had quite forgotten the Führer's predilection for talking about shit. 'Perhaps we can discuss it after the meal?' he suggests.

But Hitler talks on as if he has not heard him. 'You need to pay close attention to your stools, you know. I recommend close examination. You can dissect them and look for abnormalities. Blood. Undigested foods. Your stools tell you the health of your internal organs, you see.'

'Yes. I see,' says Bormann, although he hopes it is something he will never see.

'Do you know what Socrates said?' asks Hitler.

Bormann shakes his head.

'He said that an unexamined life is not worth living.'

Bormann wonders if this is one of the Führer's rare attempts at humour, and if he should laugh, or if the Führer is serious, in which case it would be quite inappropriate. And then a sudden thought comes to him, quite unbidden, of the Führer suddenly saying, 'Come!' and making him follow him into the toilet so he can shit for him and show him how to examine it. There had been talk about the Führer's sexual obsessions, of course, as there had been so much talk that tried to malign his greatness. But he can't imagine Eva Braun ever participating in anything so vulgar. She was far too…he searches for the word.

'If you are having trouble with your stools, you must tell me immediately,' says the Führer, 'and I can prepare some special meals for you. It is not too much bother. Men at our age need to ensure their bowels are free.'

'Fibre *macht Frei*,' says Bormann.

But Hitler pays his feeble joke no attention. 'A healthy stool is a sign of a healthy body.'

'Yes, of course,' says Bormann, and he suddenly remembers something that the fat jester Göring had mumbled, after the Führer had given a similar discourse at a staff meeting. 'But is such an obsession with healthy stools the sign of a healthy mind?' He is glad that he had been able to see Göring demoted as a traitor. Glad that he'd organised for the potassium cyanide to be delivered to his jail cell. Though perhaps he should have let him hang himself on his shoelaces like common criminals did. He'd read somewhere, though he couldn't recall where, that when you were hanged you shat yourself. Yes, that would have been more fitting. Then the investigators could have sifted through his shit to see the state of his fear-filled bowels.

Bormann thinks it time to manoeuvre a change in the conversation. He points at the screen and says, 'How many ships have the British lost already?'

And Hitler says, 'Seven badly damaged or sunk, by my tally. They are fools to announce it to the world of course. The Argentinian intelligence agents need only switch on their televisions to know the extent of enemy losses. But you'll notice that the Argentinians aren't publicising their losses in this way. It's bad for morale.'

Bormann watches the footage of aircraft flying over the bleak islands. The reception is so poor it looks like they are flying in a snow storm. 'But the British announce all their major victories as well,' he says.

'Fools,' says Hitler. 'And what is the benefit of that? All they are doing is setting themselves up for over-extending their offensives, falsely believing they have the Argentinians on the run. When the counter-offensive comes, their defences will crumble before it.' Hitler fixes his eyes on Bormann and says, 'History teaches us that.'

'Of course,' says Bormann, seeing the Führer is working up a head of steam.

'We learned this lesson ourselves harshly in the First World War. Do you remember after our last great offensive in 1918 how the newspapers were crowing that we had the Allies on the run, and how our storm-trooper tactics were over-running their lines?' He pauses between mouthfuls of mashed vegetables. 'Even I was caught up in the euphoria, wishing to be back in the front lines. But I was on sick leave at the time, after being gassed in action.'

And Bormann cannot prevent himself from casting a quick glance at Blondi.

'The newspapers kept telling us how our troops would be in Paris any day. Can you imagine how it felt to be there in hospital, out of the action, after so many years of stalemate, to think that our comrades were striding over French soil, driving all opposition before them? We had barely dared dream of such things in the trenches. And now it was coming true, and some of us weren't a part of it. It made us exuberant and it made us somewhat bitter as well.' He looks down into his mashed vegetables. 'We found out the truth from a hospital pastor, who came in one day, distressed, to tell us that our lines had collapsed everywhere and the German high command had capitulated. Now we really knew what bitterness was. We had been betrayed on all sides. By the newspapers. By the generals. By the communists within. By the Jews!'

Hitler is holding his fork like a microphone now and waving his other hand in the air in a fist. 'We had lost the Great War. A great victory was turned into a great defeat in front of us. Our soldiers had been betrayed. Those of us sacrificing ourselves on the altar of German sovereignty, had been betrayed. And that became the catalyst for National Socialism. The realism that we had to purge the state and the nation. Had to clean it out from the inside so that we could continue that great advance into Paris. So that we could complete what had been undone. *Sieg Heil!*'

'*Sieg Heil,*' replies Bormann, throwing his arm up in a Nazi salute, and struggling to his feet. In doing so, he tips some of his mash onto the floor. '*Mein Führer,*' says Bormann. 'I apologise. It is the fervour of the moment that seized me.'

Hitler waves Bormann back down to the couch with his fork. 'Sit. Sit,' he says. 'You must not upset your digestion.'

'*Jawohl, mein Führer,*' says Bormann and sits back down. He watches Blondi step across and sniffs the food he has spilled, but turns her nose up at it.

'I have more,' says the Führer and reaches out for the Tupperware container on the small coffee table before them.

'*Danke,*' says Bormann, and tries once more to turn the subject away from matters digestive. 'Do you think the Americans will come to the aid of the British?' he says, pointing at the television screen. 'They have a history of it.'

'That is an interesting question,' the Führer says, placing the Tupperware container back on the coffee table. 'But I think you'll find that history teaches us that America is ruled more by self-interest, and in this case President Reagan will undoubtedly find himself torn between his love of all things British, such as Queen Elizabeth and Mrs Thatcher, and his determination to rid the world of communism.'

And once again Bormann has an unbidden vision in his mind of Margaret Thatcher, dressed in Germanic opera helmet and spear, with leather bustiere, in bed with Ronald Reagan, who is strapping a saddle to her and then waving his Stetson in the air. It is not a pretty image, he thinks. He is getting tired and should be in bed, where such images are just bad dreams.

'And I believe that if it came to a choice of saving an ally, or saving America from the communist menace, Herr Reagan will have no option but to align himself with the South Americans, who are also avowed anti-communists.'

Martin Bormann nods in consideration.

'Think about it,' says Hitler. 'Mrs Thatcher is proving herself an opponent of socialism, it is true. But not an active force against communism. How many union leaders has she thrown from helicopters? How many left-leaning journalists has she kidnapped in the night and tortured? The Americans are nowadays more are more aligned ideologically with us, and they will prefer to see an extreme right victory. The battle for the Falklands will determine a new global political alignment of power. The Argentinian victory will be the first step in a re-emergence of military regimes. You see the importance of it all?'

And now, for the first time, Bormann does see it. He had thought it a minor skirmish that was all about political egos. Two unpopular regimes trying to whip up populist support. A battle between two bald men over a comb, as he had heard it described. But now that the

Führer has said it, he sees how it could clearly be part of a much larger strategy. And yet…and yet…he thinks.

'Look,' says Hitler, pointing at the television screen. 'Another score of British have surrendered!'

But to Bormann it seems that through the snow of the fuzzy TV reception they look more like Argentinians standing there with their arms above their heads.

Bormann is back in the bunker, in those last terrible days of the war. He is hurrying down the corridors to get the Führer. To stop him from shooting himself. To convince him that if they left now they could escape. Could start all over again. But the corridors seem unfamiliar to him. The metal cabinets and desks are all in different places. And there is a constant stream of soldiers rushing past him in panic. Papers are strewn all over the floor and drawers have been emptied haphazardly everywhere. Soldiers with their arms full of trivial things push past him like a long line of refugees. He shouts at them to move out of his way. He glares at them and orders them to step aside. But it is as if the power of his position means nothing any more. So he pushes his way against them, looking for the corridor that will take him down the curved staircase to the lower level of the bunker where the Führer's chambers are.

But he is in a maze. The corridors turn left and right and then back on themselves, and he cannot find the stairs anywhere. At one point he sees the thin staircase that leads up the Reich Chancellery, but he doesn't even consider taking it and escaping out of the chaos about him. Not without the Führer.

He walks past the staircase and then stops and looks back from the next corner and it is gone. Then he realises that he is in a dream. That is the only explanation for it. He is walking the maze of corridors as he has done so many times before. And he tries to concentrate on how the dream goes. Tries to will it differently. Tries to impose his will to change it. To bring him to the staircase that will take him down a level to where his Führer is sitting on a couch in his chambers with Eva Braun by his side. Toying with his pistol and a capsule of poison. He must reach him before he takes it. Must find the stairs before he hears the distant crack of the pistol firing a bullet into the Führer's head.

He is in empty rooms now. Long deserted of fleeing soldiers. Dust is already thick on the floors. The Russian pigs have pissed in the corners and have smashed anything they were able. But they haven't found the stairs down to the lower level of the bunker. He is certain of that. The Führer is still down there. He steps into another room, so like all the others he has walked through. The three concrete walls are bare, and when he turns back there is a fourth concrete wall behind him too. There is no door in any of the walls.

He looks up and then looks at the floor. '*Nein*!' he shouts and pounds the walls with his hands. He slams into each wall in turn, hoping his bulk will somehow move it, or shatter it, but it is unresisting. He will need to will his way free. Will his way down into the lower level to save the Führer. He is sure he can do it. Sure he can if he tries hard enough. But he feels himself slipping into blackness. Like drowning. He tries to conjure up light and a path out of the cell, but feels himself sinking into the soft cloying grip of the darkness.

Fünf

The broad masses of a population are more amendable
to the appeal of rhetoric than to any other force.

– *Mein Kampf*

Bormann is woken the next morning at ten a.m. sharp by the sound of the Führer's toilet flushing above him. The pipes in the house rattle as the water and waste runs down the pipes next to his head. He closes his eyes a moment as he feels the last traces of a dream slipping away from him. He tries to catch the details of it, but all he retains is an ominous sense of foreboding. If he needs to extricate himself from any disfavour, he must remember to tell the Führer what an honour it is to have his bowel movements pass so close to him, he thinks.

After fifteen minutes of huffing and puffing and several loud farts, he abandons all attempts at emulating his leader, and dresses and drags himself upstairs. His knees, at eighty-two years old, aren't what they used to be and he has to massage them when he reaches to top of the stair case.

'Aha, *Guten Morgen*,' says the Führer. 'Awake at last!'

'Yes,' says Bormann. 'I slept well.'

'There is plenty of time to sleep after you are dead,' says Hitler. 'Come. I am late for my work.'

Bormann thinks both these statements odd. Firstly Hitler was a renowned deep sleeper who refused to be disturbed, so much so that the Allied invasion of Normandy was many hours progressed before he learned of it and approved a counter-attack. The generals, who feared the Allied invasion, were more afraid of waking Hitler. And as to the second statement, he can only respond to with a single word. 'Work?'

'Come,' says Hitler. 'It's not too far. We will walk.'

The first thought that strikes Bormann is that perhaps the Führer actually has an occasional menial job, like he himself has needed to do, to supplement the remains of his meagre savings. But the idea seems too preposterous to even imagine. While he has picked fruit and sold vacuum cleaners and real estate, he cannot imagine the Führer doing so.

He fetches his shoes and hat and makes his painful way back down the stairs, and then follows his leader down the hill towards the dark ocean, which is turbulent today with low grey clouds hanging over it. He considers that the ocean there before him stretches over half the globe, running all the way to South America. And he wonders for a moment if they have the same low grey sky there today as they have here. Then he is hurrying to catch up to Hitler, who seems in very high spirits and good health this morning, leading a cracking pace for his age.

The two men turn right at a service station and enter the main street. Bormann sees the large white ship's masts that adorn the centre of the road. The two men walk past a few desultory surfies standing outside the milk bar and step into the newsagency. There is an aged lady with died blue hair behind the counter, smoking heavily. Hitler picks up a copy of the *Daily Mirror*, with a large photo of a British warship on the cover, and takes it to the counter.

Bormann is dazzled by the quantity of signs and packages all crammed about the small counter, like sandbags around an entrenchment. Lottery tickets and cigarettes and lollies and back issues of part-publications and jigsaw puzzles and old paperbacks and pen refills and rude cards kept out of reach of children and matches and mini horoscopes and bubble gum cards and caps and a handwritten notice saying no change will be given for the public phone without purchasing something and matchbox cars and *Best Bets* and maps of the town.

'Good morning, Mrs Dubrovic,' Hitler says.

'Good morning, Mister Schicklgruber,' she replies as she takes his money for the newspaper and then asks, 'Seen my terrier Rexie around?'

'Not another one missing?' he asks, his eyebrows raised high, as if in actual concern.

Mrs Dubrovic turns and indicates a row of posters on her window. There are five photocopied 'Missing' notices for small dogs. Three with photos on them.

And Hitler says to Bormann, 'We seem to be losing a lot of dogs in the neighbourhood lately. It is all very mysterious.'

'It's a crime,' says Mrs Dubrovic.

'It's certainly a mystery,' he says.

And Bormann, who feels obliged to say something useful, says, 'I have read somewhere that many dogs disappear for no reason, and then, just as suddenly, they return, many days later.'

'Ah, forgive me for being rude,' says Hitler, indicating Bormann. 'This is an old colleague of mine, come to visit me, Martin, ah – I mean Josef…Josef…'

'Josef Lukas,' says Bormann quickly.

'Just so,' says Hitler. 'We are old comrades.'

'It's good to have visitors,' says Mrs Dubrovic.

'It certainly is,' says Hitler. Then he rolls his newspaper up, tucks it under one arm, makes as if to leave, and then considers something a moment and says, 'I don't want to make trouble, but I have heard Mr Luc saying that it is you who has been stealing the dogs.'

'Me?' she splutters, dropping her cigarette on the Lotto forms and having to smack at them quickly so as not to start a fire.

'Yes. He is telling people around town that you are doing it to make him look bad. He is saying that you have been stealing the dogs and then telling everybody that he catches them and cooks them up to eat them.'

'He's been saying that?' she asks.

'Yes. He has.'

'The yellow devil!' She fumbles in her cardigan pocket for another cigarette and lights it. 'I'll bet he's been eating them,' she says. 'Those Vietnamese eat dogs, you know.'

Hitler gives her a sympathetic shake of his head.

'My poor little Rexie,' she says.

'These Asians,' says Hitler. 'They're not like us, are they? It's the Mongol blood!'

'The wretch,' she says. 'I won't be buying another single sausage from him!'

'Perhaps you should not,' says Hitler.

'But his cuts are cheaper than the mini mart,' she says. She puts her cigarette in her mouth and wrings her hands. 'It's a predicament,' she says. 'I'd burn out his shop, but it would upset my customers who shop there.'

'I'm sure you'll think of something appropriate,' says Hitler.

'Yes, yes, I'm sure I will,' she says and glares into the distance.

'Well, we must be getting on,' says Hitler.

'You'd want to keep a close eye on your dog,' she says.

'Thank you for your advice,' he says. Then with a twist of his head he indicates for Martin Bormann to follow him.

They walk out of the shop and then continue down past the hairdresser and the chemist to the butcher. Hitler steps in and the bell over the door rings.

Mr Luc is standing behind the counter carving meat. He glances up at the two old men and keeps cutting. He has a large cleaver in one hand and a small carcass of some beast in the other. He trims quickly and expertly, bringing the cleaver down in a rolling motion that slices through the meat easily. He gives the men the short contemptuous glance he saves for all avowed vegetarians.

The two men stand there and observe his skill for some time. Bormann looks around the interior of the shop. There are posters showing the carcasses of sheep and cows, marking up where the different cuts come from. The air in the shop is chill and has a taste of what he can only describe as bloodied meat to it. He is surprised the Führer is tolerating it, as he's always said the smell of raw meat was nauseating to advanced sensibilities like his own.

The butcher stops chopping, he looks up and says, in heavily accented English, 'Can I help you?'

'Well, actually, I was thinking of helping you,' says Hitler, his own accent just as strong.

'Oh. What way?'

'I don't want to cause trouble or anything,' says Hitler, 'but I've just been in the newsagency.'

Mr Luc stands there with the cleaver raised in one hand. 'Yes?'

'It's about the missing dogs.'

Mr Luc doesn't say anything. Just stands there.

'Mrs Dubrovic is still saying that you have been killing the dogs in the town to sell as prime meat,' Hitler says.

Mr Luc's cleaver strikes the cutting table heavily and he has to tug to remove it. He cuts at the carcass in front of him more fiercely now, making less of a neat job of it. Then he curses and brings his cleaver down right through the middle of it, cutting bones in a quick crunch. 'She is witch!' he says. 'She tell everybody that I kill and cook missing dogs. It is not true.'

'No, of course not,' says Hitler. 'Some dogs just disappear for no reason. I've heard that said just recently.'

'Why she say this about me?'

Hitler shrugs. 'Well, she's a Croatian. They're all a bit mad. They're not like us, are they?'

Mr Luc calms himself a little at these words. 'You are good man,' he says to Hitler. 'You understand me. I come to this country to work hard and make good life. Not to make trouble.'

'Nobody wants trouble,' says Hitler. Then he asks, 'What are you cutting there? It looks very tender.'

'This will now be something special that I prepare for Mrs Dubrovic. Very special meal for her.' And he brings the cleaver down heavily again and again. Bones crunch and splinter, mixing into the meat.

'Well, good day then,' says Hitler.

The two men walk back up the road at a leisurely pace, and Bormann sees a smile of contentment upon his Führer's face.

'*Bien trabajo de mañana*, I think they'd say in Buenos Aires,' says Hitler.

Martin Bormann doesn't think he's gotten the expression quite right, but says, 'Yes. A good morning's work indeed.'

Just after lunchtime, and after the postman has been and bypassed the house and Hitler has said, 'No news from Mengele today but I am expecting a message from him any day now,' he says to Bormann, 'Come. I want to show you something.'

The two men have been sitting around the dining table as Hitler has gone through the day's newspaper, clipping the stories of the Falklands war and then spreading them around his maps, examining them carefully as if they were briefings from the front lines. Bormann, who would rather be having a nap, has tried to read the ruined remains of the newspaper, but there is not enough coherence left in it except the sports pages.

'Listen to this,' says Hitler, holding up a page he has clipped from the newspaper. 'You must seize the day. Your initiatives will be rewarded.'

Bormann looks across and sees he has the newspaper's horoscope pages.

'It is a good omen,' he tells Bormann. 'I never undertake military action without consulting the stars, you know.'

'It is good to see you keeping your military mind sharp,' Bormann says. 'But I still worry about this fight with the council that is brewing. I'm sure you will defeat them, but this is a delicate time and it might not be the best moment for declaring war just now.'

Hitler snorts out his nose and says, 'You are starting to sound like one of my generals.' Then, 'Here. Read it for yourself!' He tosses the page to Bormann, who instead looks for his own star sign – Gemini. It says, 'Caution may be advised in the face of a challenge. Lucky number 6 and lucky colour orange.'

He frowns at that for some time and then looks up at Hitler and says, 'It is your personal safety I have in mind.'

And that is when Hitler says, 'Come. I have something very interesting to show you.'

'Where are we going?' Bormann asks. 'My knees are sore.'

'Not far,' says Hitler. 'Just into the backyard.'

Bormann smiles. They can walk directly into the backyard with only a few steps, as the property is on a slope. From the back door he sees the offending shed. It is large enough for two cars, and the bright silver shines even on overcast days, he sees.

The two old men make their way up the yard, through knee-high untended grass.

'Watch out for snakes,' Hitler says.

'What type of snakes?' Bormann asks, looking around his feet.

'A snake is a snake,' says Hitler. 'You kill them and then ask questions later.'

Bormann, who has never asked a snake a question in his life, nods and says, '*Jawohl!*'

Hitler leads Bormann to a door near the back of the garage and, before unlocking it, he peers over his neighbour's fence. Bormann sees the fence is an aged paling thing and has a very obviously dog leg in it where it has been moved to extend Hitler's property line to accommodate the shed.

'The Pole is not outside today,' the Führer says. 'Some days he is in the garden, but if he sees me coming he scurries back inside like the cowardly *Untermensch* that he is.'

Hitler struggles with the large padlock on the garage door with his trembling fingers for some moments and then lifts it free. 'Come,' he says to Bormann with a slight sound of playful mystery in his voice, as if he has a big surprise, fitting for his former secretary and the former leader of the Reich Chancellery.

Inside, the shed is dusty and dark. There are no lights and Bormann sees it appears to be filled with old garden junk. Lawnmowers and other machines.

'Secret weapons?' he jokes and the Führer fixes him with a stare.

'Very perceptive!' he says. 'I underestimate you.'

Bormann steps closer to the old machinery and tries to get a closer look at it, and sees a whole row of fox traps in a box, that look like they have traces of blood and fur on them, but Hitler is beckoning him to follow him to the far side of the shed where there is a long workbench set against the wall.

'Come,' he tells him once more.

Again he fiddles with a large padlock and then Bormann notices that there is a door in the solid sides of the bench. Hitler picks up a torch and shines it down a set of stairs. And Martin Bormann has a sudden sense of déjà vu. He feels a little giddy. Feels a touch of that dream he had been having this morning. He recalls that he was in the bunker and Hitler was with him, and the bunker was collapsing about them and they were trying to get out and poor Eva was crying and Blondi was dead and…

'Come,' Hitler says once more, insistent this time.

And Bormann cannot but follow the leader he has sworn a lifelong oath of loyalty to. He bends low and climbs under the bench, descending the concrete stairs into the bunker there below. Hitler then turns a switch and the room burst into light like a bomb going off. And Bormann recognises it at once. It is so many rooms he has been in before. If Hitler's house is like his Bavarian residence, then this is like his other two headquarters. It is the conference room at the Wolf's Lair in Rastenburg, Prussia. It is the briefing room in the Reich Chancellery bunker in Berlin. It is a room filled with the taste of dampness and concrete dust. It has the smell of men's sweat and dog. Concrete chips will fall from the ceiling when a shell explodes close above and the walls will echo when women or children scream in their final fright. It is the room of so many of his nightmares.

He puts one arm out to support himself, suddenly short of breath, but the Führer does not notice. He walks across the large trestle tables spread out and holds his arms wide. 'This is my domain,' he says. 'This is the centre of history and the centre of the world.'

Bormann does not understand what the Führer is talking about and he has to close his eyes and wait for his heart to calm a little. He takes deep slow breaths and tries to conjure an image of Victoria Principal from the television show *Dallas*, in one of her skimpy tops. That always calms him.

When he opens his eyes it is no better, though. There, spread out on the table in front of him is a tactical map of Berlin. Red arrows and models show where the Russian troops pressed upon the city from the east working to encircle it, and grey arrows and models represent the German forces. It brings back those last terrible days of Berlin, when nobody knew exactly where the Russians were and whether the last escape routes were cut off or not. Every day they were told was likely to be the last day that they could escape from the city, and he remembers how Hitler has exhorted him to go, until that very last day, on the eve of the Führer's fifty-sixth birthday, when it was still possible for him to escape, he suddenly forbade him from leaving. Insisted he remain in the bunker with him until the end. Told him that he was surrounded by traitors like Göring and Himmler and could trust nobody but him. He was filled with both pride and fear.

He puts his hand to his mouth, feeling he is about to vomit. Feels the bunker swaying as if a direct hit had just landed on it.

'Look at the future,' says Hitler.

But Bormann can see only the dizzying shaking of the walls about him. 'I'm sorry,' he says, as he had so wished to say almost forty years ago. 'I cannot stay.'

And he drags himself back up the stairs, striking his head on the underside of the work bench and he staggers back out through the shed to the daylight. He staggers to the fence and vomits up all the fear and bad memories that had swollen up inside him, in the form of the mashed vegetables he had consumed for lunch. Then he falls to the ground and closes his eyes, breathing in the fresh scent of grass and sunlight and everything they all mourned for in all those months in the bunker.

'Excuse me,' says a voice.

Bormann looks up and sees nobody. Then he turns his head and sees an elderly man peering at him from over the fence.

'You have thrown up on my property.'

'You are the Pole!' Bormann says, seeing an aged man's balding head peering at him from over the wooden fence.

'I am Mister Dikowski,' the man says.

'Go to hell,' says Bormann. 'You Polish scum.'

'I will report this to the council,' says Mister Dikowski, sticking his chin out indignantly. And Martin Bormann, whom many have rightly accused of cowardly tendencies over the years, drags himself to his feet and stares the man down, saying something he has always wanted to say, since first hearing J.R. Ewing say it on television, 'I do unto others before they do unto me.'

Mr Dikowski understands the tone more than the meaning and he turns and hurries back inside the house, assuming this man is just as deranged and dangerous as his neighbour.

Later, Bormann is sitting on the Führer's balcony, imagining how easily the days could pass in peace here in Eden. The winter weather has a pleasant chill to it, unlike the interior of Brazil or the northern provinces of Argentina. It reminds him of European autumns. And he finds that staring out over the Pacific Ocean is quite hypnotic. All he has to do to prolong this sense of tranquillity is to keep his news to himself. And why should he not? He is an old man and deserves some peace at this end of his life. Surely. If only the world would cease from incessantly turning at a different pace than it appears to.

And his mind wanders off across the Pacific Ocean towards the distant Falkland Islands, where he knows men are fighting and dying, perhaps also wishing they were in such a remote haven as Eden. The TV and newspapers will show hardly any of the actual fighting, he knows. They will concentrate on distant images of planes and tanks, but in the front lines men will be stumbling through the freezing rain, running up boggy hillsides, bare of any cover, as mortar bombs drop around them, or snipers send bullets pinging about their heads.

It is a real war, he knows, with all the logistics and weaponry and death and dying of a real war – but somehow, because of the way it is being played out on the television, it seems more like some BBC drama.

And Bormann finds he is suddenly imagining he is there in the Falklands. Something he used to do from the safety of Berlin. Imagine himself on the Russian front. Or on the beaches of Normandy. Behind a machine gun lining up Allied soldiers in his sights. Some nights he lay there in bed, saving battles that had been lost. Turning around withdrawals into advances. He used to think of it afterwards as hopeless daydreaming, but knows that at the time he was gripped by a fervour so strong that he really believed he could have made a difference if he had been there.

And now he is in the Falklands, instructing the Argentinians how to set out their defences. Where to position their men and their missiles to prevent the British from gaining superiority. Every helicopter the British sent in on a scouting mission would be shot down. Commandos would be ambushed. Every assault on a beach would be met by soldiers in hiding. And then, he realises that he doesn't actually know if there are even beaches on the Falklands. He is transposing the beaches of Normandy onto the southern Atlantic islands. Those French beaches that he only ever imagined anyway, based on photographs and maps. And he supposes that, pathetic as his daydreams are, they are little better than the daydreams of the Argentinian generals who are directing the defensive war, who have also never seen the beaches of the Falklands. He is about to extend that analogy to that of the German High Command in Berlin, but draws back, as if he has just seen a landmine under his foot. Safer to imagine winning the war in the Falklands to that.

Hitler rouses Bormann from his daydreaming and tells him that they must go to buy some herbal medicines from a supplier he has on the outskirts of town. 'There are many of these people who call themselves alternative,' he tells Bormann. 'Perhaps they come here for the name. Perhaps they are just attracted to the coastal life. They are quite decadent, of course, but among them you can find skilled astrologers and those who practise herbal remedies. Look here,' he says, and he points to a small circled charm hanging over one window. It has red thread woven around a circular frame and has feathers tied into the thread and a single piece of crystal in the centre. 'Do you know what it is?'

And Bormann has to admit that he does not.

'It is a dream catcher!' says Hitler. 'Can you imagine that? It was created by North American Indians, but of course this one was made for me by a handsome young woman with blonde hair. Quite Aryan really. And here,' he says, leading Bormann back inside and indicating the sideboard, 'these boxes contain crystals that channel different energies. There is a small shop about thirty minutes' drive north of here. You can use them to focus your life force more effectively.'

Bormann says he should like to try them some time.

'Yes,' says the Führer. 'You shall. And I will take you to visit a woman who does rune castings. Do you know what that is?'

And Bormann has to admit that he does not.

'It is like the Tarot,' Hitler says, 'but it uses small stones with runic inscriptions carved on them. The Celtic people used them in ancient days, and they are closely related to the Aryans. Come,' says Hitler. 'We shall both have our fortunes cast today.'

After dithering around the house for a few minutes, collecting keys and his hat and so on, he leads Blondi and Bormann out the front of the house where a very aged and rusted green Volkswagen sits in the driveway. 'You will need to sit in the back with Blondi,' Hitler says. 'The passenger side door no longer opens.'

Bormann looks at the vehicle apprehensively. It looks as old as the two men, but the Führer tips the bucket seat forward and says, 'Come. Come.'

Bormann hops in the back seat, positioning himself between the splits in the vinyl where springs and stuffing can be seen. He looks down to his feet and sees the driveway through a few rusted holes there.

'Ready?' asks the Führer, climbing in and turning the key in the ignition. Nothing happens. Hitler mutters a little and tries again. 'Nothing to be concerned about,' he says and lets the handbrake off.

The car starts rolling slowly down the driveway, backwards.

Hitler steers them awkwardly out onto the road and then uses their momentum to turn them around so they are facing down the hill. 'Contact!' he says and rolls forward.

Bormann can see the dark asphalt of the road rushing beneath his feet as Hitler works the clutch to jump-start the Volkswagen. It jerks once. Then again. Then it fires and with a belch of smoke and a strong smell worse than Blondi the engine kicks into life.

'It is going to be an auspicious day,' Hitler calls back over his shoulder. 'I can feel it.'

Bormann looks out towards the ocean and sees the sun is now shining down on it, turning it a deep blue. Hitler turns into a side street, drives around the block and the car struggles back up the hill, then turns south.

They drive through thick forests for perhaps ten minutes and then Bormann sees a ravaged landscape outside the window like a war zone. The earth is turned up as if a major artillery barrage has fallen here and there are only the straggly remains of a few trees left.

'*Mein Gott!*' he says. 'What happened here?'

'The Garden of Eden,' says Hitler. 'They cut the trees to make wood chips. There are many foresters here, but also many green protesters. It is a war zone between them sometimes.'

Soon they are driving through forests again and Bormann has just started to relax a little when he hears the siren wail behind them. Hitler looks up into the rear-view mirror and curses. Bormann tries to turn his head around to see what it is, as Hitler pulls the car over the edge of the road. Now he can manage it and sees there is a police car behind them. Hitler is gripping the steering wheel tightly and cursing still.

Bormann watches a policeman emerge from the car and walk up to the driver's door.

He looks in and shakes his head. 'Mr Schicklgruber,' he says in a weary voice, 'I thought we had a little talk about you driving.'

Hitler waves his hand as if dismissing a pesky insect.

'Or have you had your licence reinstated and your car miraculously registered since our last encounter?'

Hitler acts as if he cannot hear him.

'If anybody could actually call this a car,' the policeman says. 'Let me see if I can recall. Bald tyres. No working lights. Unsafe exhaust leaking into the cab. Non-functional windscreen wipers.'

'It is not raining,' mutters Hitler.

But the policeman keeps shaking his head. 'I'm afraid this time I'm going to have to impound your vehicle and escort you back home in mine.'

'It is an outrage!' says Hitler. 'My friend here is a war veteran and we are going to seek medical assistance for him. Would you imperil his life?'

The policeman looks in the back seat at Martin Bormann, who smiles back at him. 'Then let's take him past the local hospital on our way back to your place,' he says.

And so it is that the two aged men spend the next hour at the local hospital, where Martin Bormann is, at the policeman's suggestion, subject to all manner of undignified tests. Then, late in the day, the two men are returned to Hitler's home in the police car. Hitler climbs out, head held high, as if he was stepping out of the gates after his first sojourn in prison in 1922 to an adoring crowd. Martin Bormann sees the woman in the house across the road peeping at them from between her venetian blinds.

The policeman tells them they should both be gratified that Mr Lukas here is in such good health for a man his age, and that he hopes he does not catch Mr Schicklgruber out on the road again, unless it is in a wheelchair or a taxi. The Führer curses him in mumbled German. Bormann is silent. The results of the blood tests will be back in two or three days and will confirm what he has known for some time. But he does not want the Führer to know it. He was always untrusting of those with malignant diseases. Even though his own mother had died of a malignant breast cancer that had spread throughout her body. As if it were a sign of betrayal. And Bormann often feels his own body has betrayed him. Turned on him. Plotting his death cell by cell.

Hitler waits until the policeman has driven off and then says aloud, 'Fascist!' before realising what he has said. Then he turns to Martin Bormann and says, 'It just proves that the people will more readily believe a big lie than a small one. I did not tell a big enough lie. Next time we are caught you will be the president of Hungary, travelling incognito in Australia.'

The two men go upstairs and Hitler slumps into his chair. 'Now we will not have our fortunes told,' Hitler says and he pulls a long face.

Bormann can see his leader is starting to sink into one of his dark moods and, to tell the truth, he feels like joining him.

Hitler sighs and then he says, 'It was all Mussolini's fault, of course. That tin-pot dictator. If he had been able to invade Greece on his own, without needing German troops to save his neck, we would not have been delayed in invading Russia by four weeks. We would have reached Moscow before the winter set in. Do you know we were only thirty kilometres from the city when we were bogged down by the snows? One day's advance perhaps. Maybe two.' He sighs and his bushy grey eyebrows sink so low that Bormann can barely see his eyes. 'We lost the war because of him. He deserved to be strung up by the heels by partisans with his mistress!'

Bormann wonders if Hitler has forgotten how shocked he was in the last days of the war, when he heard that was just how Mussolini had been captured and killed. Millions of deaths were acceptable – but the lynching of his ally was personal. He was filled with a terrible fear of the same thing happening to him by Berliners, and he went searching for potassium cyanide capsules. It was Bormann himself who had dissuaded him from taking his life at the end. Or, he wonders, is that just his own memory distorting the past too?

He looks to his Führer, who is sinking lower and lower into the chair. Blondi walks over and puts her head on his lap, but Hitler does not notice.

And then Bormann, lapsing easily into his distant role of maintaining the Führer's morale, says, 'Show me the bunker room once more. I just had a bad memory last time. But I very much want to see it.'

Hitler glances at him. 'Really?'

'Yes, of course.'

Hitler shrugs. 'Come then,' he says, and once more he leads Bormann out through the backyard to the large shed, fiddles with the locks and leads him down into the low-ceilinged room hidden underneath it.

Bormann sees that there are in fact two maps spread out on the trestle tables, side by side. The first one is that showing the Battle for Berlin but the other is a map of the English Channel, with the coastlines of France and England on it. At first he thinks it is a schematic of the invasion of Normandy, but then he sees the blue Allied models are centred on Dunkirk. But there are also grey models on the coast of England.

He walks around the table and it takes him some moments to understand it. It is the invasion of England being played out there. The British forces at Dunkirk have been completely surrounded and are obviously unable to escape across the Channel. They will be annihilated there, he can see. And at the same time the German navy has led a force across the Channel, landing on the coasts at Sandgate and near Dover. Then he sees the direction of the German advance laid out in arrows. The army will advance not directly on London, but to the west of it, encircling the city from the north while a secondary force advances up the Thames.

He turns and sees Hitler is standing on the bottom step nodding and smiling to him. 'Operation Wotan,' he says. 'The way it should have been played out.'

Bormann looks back to the table. Studies the thrusts and turns of the German troops. They outmanoeuvre the British troops by isolating the major pockets of defence and attacking London from its north.

'It is brilliant,' Bormann says. 'How long does the battle take?'

'Five weeks,' the Führer says, 'as long as the accursed English rain doesn't bog things down.'

'And what of the rest of the nation?'

'It is immaterial. Once we march through the streets of London, the war with England is effectively over. We install Sir Oswald Mosley as prime minister. Shoot Churchill if we have managed to capture him. Imprison the Royal Family or send them back to live with their German relatives under house arrest in Bavaria. And the rest of the country will throw up fortifications to defend themselves, but will never attack. We will win them over politically and economically when they have no other choice but to join the Reich.'

Bormann is speechless. 'It is how it should have been,' he says.

'It is history rewritten,' says Hitler. 'I can replay all the great battles of the war here and engineer them how they should have gone. I can win the battle for Stalingrad a dozen different ways. I can conquer North Africa and crush the British tank forces. I can repel the Allied invasion forces on the beaches of Normandy. I can take Moscow!'

'Yes,' says Bormann. 'Let us take Moscow and crush the Bolsheviks. That would be something.'

'Come then,' says Hitler and steps down the last step into the bunker. 'Let me get the map of Russia.'

Uncle and his friend are down in the secret room playing the map game. I hear them from outside and let myself in, walking quietly down the stairs and sitting there, watching them. They are both smiling. Uncle is doing the pincer attack on Stalingrad, as he likes to do, and his friend is mostly just agreeing with everything he says.

I think that Uncle's friend doesn't really understand the game, because Uncle makes several mistakes that he doesn't correct. When we play the game, I tell him when the numbers of his soldiers and the numbers of other soldiers are not in his favour, like when playing Uno. He says that boldness can make up for the numbers not being in his favour, but I have tried that when playing Uno and it doesn't always work. I tell him that if he pays attention to the numbers he will have a much better chance of winning and I show him which way he should move his troops on the map. He says he wishes that I had been one of his generals because I would have been a great help to him.

He is a good help to me too. He showed me what to do to the boys who bully me at school. I don't like school, but Mummy says I should go, except for the days she says I should stay home and look after her. Uncle says it is important to have a good education – but not to confuse wisdom and knowledge. He says many people have knowledge but not many of them have wisdom. And he says above all a person must have action. He says that knowing what to do to stop the big boys bullying me is knowledge, and knowing the right time to do it without being caught is wisdom, but actually doing it is action.

He even took me out at night, and we went to each of the bully's houses and left a message for them. He said it was important that they were divided.

At Damien McInerney's we took his bike and Uncle drove his car over it. At Mark Russo's house he threw a paper bag that smelled of poo into his bedroom window. And at Michael Johnson's we caught his cat. Its name was Tigger. Uncle put it in a sack with a rock in it and dropped in into the bay. We left a note at each house that said, 'Adam's friends are watching you!'

The boys stared at me angrily after that but they didn't bully me any more. Mark Russo caught me once inside the toilets at school and said I should tell him who my friends were or he'd flush my head down the toilet. But Uncle had already told me what to say if this happened. I told Mark Russo that I wouldn't tell him who they were, but I'd tell them he said he'd flush my head down the toilet. He swore a lot but he let me go. Just like Uncle said he would.

I watch the two men encircling the Russian troops in the map game until I see Uncle's friend make a big mistake. I say, 'The numbers of enemy are too strong there.'

Uncle looks across at me and nods a little, but Uncle's friend jumps as if I had leaped out from hiding and given him a fright.

'Where did you come from?' he asks me.

'My mother's tummy,' I tell him. That's a joke she taught me. But he doesn't laugh.

'The little general is right,' says Uncle. 'You are imperilling our forces!' Uncle's friend glares angrily at me, the way the bullies did – but he doesn't do anything else either.

Sechs

Nature…puts living creatures on this globe
and watches the free play of forces.

– Mein Kampf

Later that evening, after the two aged Nazis have thoroughly defeated the Russian forces and celebrated their victory with one more meal of reheated vegetable mash, they sit out on Hitler's veranda and look up at the stars. The breeze is a little chill, but carries the refreshing salty smell of the ocean. Hitler says he has a special treat for Bormann and he brings out a bottle with a thick orange juice in it.

'What is it?' asks Bormann.

'Carrot juice,' says Hitler. 'I brew it myself. I have many bottles of it in storage. It seems to get better with age and is also good for keeping out the cold. It is very healthy.' He pours Bormann a glass and then one for himself and says, 'Come, let us toast to the future.'

Bormann lifts his glass and says, 'To the future!' He takes a tentative sip of the carrot juice and winces. It appears to have fermented in the bottle. He looks across to Hitler, who was always ardently opposed to alcohol, and sees him down his glass in one long go, and then pour himself another.

'Come,' he says and holds up his glass to propose another toast.

Best not to tell him, he thinks.

'To fallen comrades and absent friends!' The old army toast.

'Yes,' says Bormann, 'To fallen comrades and absent friends.' And he takes a deep drink of the bitter-tasting concoction. He looks up at the bright stars and says, 'I can feel it warming me a little.'

'Then have another,' says Hitler and offers the bottle to him.

They drink in silence for a moment, and Bormann starts to feel all his anxieties dropping away. Starts to feel perhaps his Führer is right. He should not back down to the council. He should defend his property line. He should get another car and keep driving. He should not submit to the forces who are trying to imprison him. And he will stand here beside his leader and fight with him. This time he won't run away.

'Are they still searching for me in South America?' Hitler suddenly asks.

Bormann shakes his head. 'Only the madmen imagine you are still alive. Only those who are also looking for Elvis Presley and flying saucers.'

The Führer nods in satisfaction.

'For most of the world, you died in the bunker with Eva,' Bormann says. Poor Eva.

The Führer nods again. Then he says, 'I have kept a record of sightings of myself, do you know, and never once was I sighted in Australia.'

Bormann says, 'I remember the story that you had been seen living in Belgium, and I was your valet.'

'Yes,' says the Führer, ticking the sightings off on his fingers. 'And I was also seen living on a ranch in Chile. Or in northern Scotland. I was seen working as a croupier in a casino in Evian in France. I was living as a hermit in Italy. I was in a remote town in Paraguay. Even in a swamp village in Brazil.'

And now Bormann nods and giggles a little. 'And I have been seen in cafés in Buenos Aires. On a bus in Rio de Janeiro. In a hotel in Asunción in Paraguay. And do you know what – it probably *was* me they had seen.' And he laughs.

'That's nothing,' says the Führer. 'I have been seen in Burma. In China. In Cape Town and Harare. In Leningrad even! There was even a story about a secret Nazi base in Antarctica where I and many of the surviving leaders fled to. And do you know why they keep imagining I am still alive?'

'Why?'

'Because they need to keep creating me. They need to demonise me. They need to personify all the things they fear and loathe. It is my destiny,' he says.

'To destiny,' says Bormann and holds up the glass again.

'But they will never catch us,' says Hitler. 'They will never catch all of us. We have our protection, as well you know.'

And Bormann nods, but a little hesitantly.

'Klaus Barbie. Otto Albrecht. Alois Brunner. Reinhard Gehlen. They are all still drawing pay from Western security organisations, are they not?'

Bormann does not directly answer and says, 'When we arrived in Australia, there were more Nazis in the camps with us than there were refugees.'

Hitler smiles. 'I used to think the Croat *Ustashe* was a troublesome waste of energy, but they have certainly proved their worth.'

'Bishop Hudal and Father Draganovic are the only two clergy I have any respect for,' Bormann says. 'They understood that by helping us out of Europe they were preserving Christianity against the atheist forces of Bolshevism and European socialism.'

'They understood their place in history,' Hitler says.

The two men sit in silence a while, looking out into the dark past and Hitler says, 'It was all Göring's fault, of course. If he had taken more care of the state of the Luftwaffe than his own personal wardrobe and the acquisition of artworks, we would have crushed the British at Dunkirk and been victorious in the Battle of Britain. We would have sent the Russians back over the steppes.' He sighs and his shoulders sink so low it looks as if they are about to detach and fall to the floor. 'He deserved to be demoted. He was lucky I didn't have him shot.'

Bormann nods. He can remember the crafty channels that Göring had used to send his telegram to the high command in the last days of the war, asking if the rumours were true that Hitler had been incapacitated, and if that was so then he should surely take control of the Reich. Bormann had intercepted the telegram, however, and had taken it to the Führer, playing up his fear of betrayal from within. Or, he wonders, is that just how he prefers to remember it?

'I'll tell you something interesting,' he tells Hitler, to change the topic. 'You'd be surprised how many Nazis have been protected and cared for by women.'

'Mengele was always a bit of a ladies' man, I recall,' says Hitler. 'I'm sure he has a bevy of Latino beauties looking after him.'

Bormann is surprised to hear Hitler talking like this. He was always very prudish about anything at all sexual. 'Well, yes. He has known many women in South America,' he says, 'if I can use that term.'

And Hitler shakes his head. 'The man is a rogue at heart. Always was. Do you know I heard he used to keep pictures of naked Jewesses in his office at Auschwitz?'

'Yes. I heard that,' says Bormann.

'And here's a story about Himmler you won't have heard,' Hitler says. 'Do you know that he once boasted to Göring that he could bed any woman he pleased, but Göring replied that it was such a pity that he could not please any woman!' And he laughs. A single short bark that startles Blondi.

And then Bormann does something quite out of character. Perhaps it is the effect of too much fermented carrot juice. Perhaps his judgement has become a little impaired with old age. So many perhapses as to why he is less able to gauge an indiscretion. But he looks across at his leader and asks, 'Is it true what they say about Geli Raubal?'

'And what exactly do they say?' the Führer asks him.

And Bormann has begun replying before he realises that the Führer is no longer smiling. Hitler is staring at him intensely.

'They say that she was much more than your niece,' Bormann says and then falters, seeing the noose he has laid out for himself.

'And?' asks Hitler.

Bormann glances at the Führer and then looks away. Those pale blue eyes burn towards him. He licks his lips and says, 'And they say that her death was a tragedy for one so young in that…in that…' Then he says quickly, 'They say that she killed herself because her love for you would be forever unrequited.'

Hitler stares at him for some moments more and then says, 'If that is what they say, they deserve to be told the truth. She was young and she was in love with me, but I told her that my duty to the German people prevented me from ever entering a long-term relationship. It was the grief of knowing that which drove her to shoot herself.' Then he asks Bormann, 'Is that how you had believed it to be?'

And Bormann licks his lips again, with a little snake-flick of his tongue. There had been so many things said about the death of Geli Raubal, the daughter of Hitler's half-sister Angelika. It was well known that the young woman was infatuated with her step-uncle and had lived with him from late 1929 until her death in September 1931. But it was said that he kept her a prisoner in his flat in Munich. Refused to let her see anybody but himself. It was said that he practised degrading sexual activities on her. It was said that he was the one who was deeply in love with her. It was said that the party had organised the so-called suicide to save him from disgrace. It was all too neat, it was said, that she had used Hitler's own pistol to end her life, while he was many kilometres away at Nuremberg. It was also said that she had a young Jewish lover that Hitler had discovered. And it was said that Hitler had sunk into a deep and dark depression after her death. That he had never quite recovered from it. But it was also said that Hitler had only one testicle. And he suspected he had no more chance of knowing the truth of Geli's death than he did of asking Hitler to show him his testicles.

'Yes,' says Bormann. 'I had always imagined it just so.' But there were so many other things about Geli he had often imagined. He had thought of the attractive young girl bound with leather thongs as Hitler whipped her. He has imagined her wearing thin garments with her breasts poking out and being tied to the bed. He has imagined standing there in Hitler's boots waving a whip over her naked body.

For that is the real truth of things, he knows. Deep down, he has always imagined being in Hitler's boots. Pissing in Hitler's toilet. Being with Hitler's women. Even now in old age, in his near non-existence in this sleepy sanctuary at the end of the world, he cannot but think that every ingratiating step closer to the Führer that he takes allows him to be standing in his place. It is a depressing thought to come to such a realisation so late in one's life, he knows. Both to understand what has been a driving force of his life and to know that there is absolutely nothing else he can do about it. He has seen a truth of himself more than any of the old Nazi hunters had ever sighted.

But all he says is, 'Once again I am filled with unbounded admiration for my Führer's dedication to his destiny.'

And then Hitler also does something quite out of character. He asks Bormann, 'Do you know what everybody said of you in the bunker?'

Bormann shakes his head, although he suspects he knows the answer.

'They said you were a toady.' And the Führer giggles. 'They said that you were the serpent that I should be most cautious of.'

'Who said that?' asks Bormann.

'Everybody,' says Hitler.

'Who?'

'Everybody. Goebbels. Himmler. Göring. And especially Albert.'

'Albert Speer?' asks Bormann.

'No. Your brother Albert.'

Bormann's face grows dark. It has been many years since anybody spoke the name of his brother to him. The two had such a strong dislike for each other that is was necessary to organise meetings separately if there was an issue that involved both of them. In the bunker, he was Hitler's personal adjutant.

'That weasel,' says Bormann. 'That obsequious, arse-licking, power-hungry leach!'

And Hitler giggles again. 'That is just how he described you,' he says.

Bormann's face grows even darker. He had spent much of his energies in the bunker in controlling access to the Führer, making sure that he and he alone held the power of granting who should get to see the Führer and who should not. He had successfully driven Hess and Hitler apart earlier in the war. He was instrumental in having that fat coward Göring declared a traitor and demoted when he tried to assume control of the Reich in the last days. He knows he was widely loathed by the generals, and it always burns him up inside that Albert was so popular with people. Albert would get the invitations to birthday drinks or get to meet a new pretty girl or would get to hear the latest gossip. But around himself everyone became tight-mouthed and taciturn. Even after almost forty years, the name of Albert tastes bitter in his mouth.

'Do you know what happened to him?' asked Hitler. 'I have never seen his name on any documents about the final days.'

And Bormann says, 'He survived and was able to avoid both the Russian soldiers and the Allied prosecutors. Every five years or so he sends out some misinformation that I have been sighted in Brazil or Finland or Australia even. He just can't stop causing trouble for me. As soon as the Nazi hunters give up on me as dead, he starts another rumour.'

'I remember a story of a skeleton being uncovered during excavations in Berlin about a decade ago, that was identified as being you, and I presumed it was Albert.'

'I was not so fortunate,' Bormann says.

'So your hate for each other hasn't diminished?'

Bormann ponders that for a while, and then says, 'Hate is a strange emotion. You become addicted to it and it keeps you living.'

Hitler nods as if he knows this to be true. 'And you were probably the most hated man in Berlin in 1945,' he says.

And Bormann's chest swells up with pride at this as if he considers it a badge of honour. Though he is also thinking that if people could detect a person's hatred the many Nazi hunters would have tracked him down many, many years ago.

He looks up now and sees the stars have disappeared. He can't quite fathom that for a moment, then it starts raining. Slow drops that suddenly build in intensity.

'It is raining,' says Bormann. And then he turns to the Führer and says, 'Ask me what the weather is like in the Falklands tonight.'

'All right. What is the weather like in the Falklands tonight?'

And Bormann says in English, 'Hail Hitler!' He laughs and then suddenly stops.

The Führer is just staring at him. 'Is that meant to be funny?' he asks. 'Mocking me?'

'Of course not,' says Bormann humbly and thinks he had better find an excuse to retire for the night before his tongue gets him into any more trouble. Before he has to start stating what an honour it is to sleep next to the Führer's sewage downpipe. He struggles to his feet, finding it quite difficult to stand straight, and says, 'I must go downstairs now. I need to urinate quickly.'

Hitler watches him stagger inside and says, 'That's quite ambitious for a man of your age.'

Bormann is back in the bunker. Like he is on so many nights. But this time the Führer is ready. Is behind the door of his quarters, calling to him. Bormann is battering on the door, trying to force it open, bit will not budge. Then suddenly the door opens. The Führer is standing there with one hand on the door handle. He urges Bormann inside. He can see the Führer is wounded. Blood is flowing from a wound on his head. Bormann looks about and sees Eva lying on the couch, as if she were asleep there.

The Führer takes Bormann's two hands in his own and tells him that the future of the Reich now rests on his shoulders. Then he collapses in Bormann's arms. And Bormann holds him tight. Determined not to let him go. He holds him tight and wills him to live. Sees his eyes open. But he is looking into his own face. Bormann has become the Führer. At last. As he was always destined to. He steps out of the room, leaving the two bodies behind, and looks left and right. The corridor is a maze. But he wills it to return to the familiar design of the bunker. Wills it to return to order.

He steps into the guards' room and sees Mrs Thatcher there, dressed in a bronze bustiere like one of Wagner's Valkyries, She beckons him to her, her busts heaving. It is the power of being the Führer. If he wills it, he can have Mrs Thatcher and Victoria Principal both. He can create a golden stairwell and ascend out of the bunker. Can rally the German troops to drive back the Russians. Can will a victory out of defeat.

The room around him moves. Mrs Thatcher is gone. He is in the four-walled empty room again. He places his hands against the walls and concentrates. Wills a door to appear there. Then steps into the next room. It is identical. He turns back and the door is gone. He walks to the far wall and places his hand against that too. Concentrates and wills another door to appear. He must hurry, he thinks. For the Russians are getting closer and he needs to rally the German soldiers before they are wiped out. He must will himself free of these cells.

He goes through the door. He is in a third room. Again with no door. He goes to the far wall and places his hands against it. Concentrates. Passes into the next room. And the next. And the next. Places his hands against the far wall of each room and brings his will to bear against the forces trying to imprison him. For this is what it is to be the Führer.

Sieben

Fate must bring retribution, unless men conciliate fate while there is still time.

– Mein Kampf

Martin Bormann creeps up the darkened staircase slowly. Years of caution have taught him how to move without making any sound. Ever since Eichmann was captured, he's never slept soundly. If you drop off too deeply, the Israelis would have a dark hood over your head and have you bundled into a car before you could shake the sleep from your eyes.

Something has woken him, and he feels a sense of unease filling him. There is a bitter sour taste in his stomach, that he first mistakes for ill-boding. But when he finds that his feet do not step as carefully as he wishes them to, he curses that infernal carrot wine. He can see there is a light on upstairs in the living room, and he can hear strange voices. At least two of them. He has already checked the time; it is after three a.m. So many thoughts run through his mind. Burglars? The Wiesenthal gang? Who knows, maybe even ASIO? Stranger things have happened. He wishes he had his old war Luger with him.

He suddenly no longer wishes to be the Führer. He knows that whatever torment his captors have in mind for him, it is something he could never endure. And he would never be able to beg and grovel for mercy as a Führer. The status of office would not allow it. He must now confront whoever is in the house and beg and grovel for himself and for his leader. He must protect him.

He reaches the top of the stairs and peeks around the corner. He sees Hitler sitting there at the table, working busily at something, muttering in Spanish. Then he hears the second voice more clearly now, and he understands. There is a language record playing. Hitler is learning Spanish and repeating the voice of the record.

Then Hitler says, without even turning around, 'Come in, Bormann, I want to show you something.'

Bormann sheepishly approaches, not wishing to have appeared so fearful about nothing, and Hitler bids him turn off the record player. He does and then sits opposite Hitler, who still does not look up. Bormann sees he has hundreds of small scraps of newspaper spread out on the table and he is moving them into columns and then moving them into other ones, as if he is completing a large jigsaw puzzle.

'What is it?' asks Bormann eventually.

And now the Führer does look up at him, with a look something like admonishment because Bormann does not recognise what he's doing. Although in answer, Hitler only picks up one of the small pieces of newspaper and passes it to him. Bormann takes it and reads it carefully. It says, 'Aries: Things are looking up. Watch for prosperity about you. Lucky number 7. Best colour red.'

He reads it two or three times and then passes it back. Hitler sees that he still doesn't understand and passes him another. It says, 'Aries: Beware sudden misfortune today. Avoid surprise invitations. Lucky number 4. Best colour white.'

Bormann looks up and sees Hitler nodding at him, as if needing him to understand. But his head is too foggy. He is still not thinking clearly. And so he says, 'Horoscopes.' He's always thought that a strange word in English. Horoscopes – scopes of horror! And there are years of horoscopes, collected from tabloids and magazines, laid out before them.

'Yes,' says Hitler triumphantly. He picks up another one, examines it carefully and then lays it down in one column.

Bormann watches him for some moments and then asks, 'How do you know which column to put them in?'

'Aha,' says Hitler, as if Bormann has finally asked a question worth addressing seriously. 'That's where divination comes in. You see, taken individually, these horoscopes provide a small fraction of a life, but if you put them all together, you get a much broader picture. A larger canvas. If you lay them all out sequentially, you can read the story of a man's life in them.' Then he pauses and holds up one finger. 'But, what might happen if you re-arranged them into a new order. Just the right precise order?'

Bormann thinks carefully before answering. 'You could rewrite a man's past?' he says.

Hitler gives a look of exasperation. 'You think too narrow,' he says. 'You need to open your mind to possibilities. That is the mark of a visionary. Think of this: if you were to rearrange them in just the right order, the one correct order, might it not be like breaking a code, like a cipher of life, that could be determine your long-term future?'

Bormann thinks hard on this. He wonders if he's just too tired to grasp what the Führer is trying to teach him. Wonders if it will make more sense in the morning. Hitler passes him another clipping. This one reads, 'Aries: Make your own fortune. Set your path and follow it. Lucky number 20. Best colour red or black.'

Bormann reads it twice and says, 'So if you can get these all in the right order...'

'Exactly,' says Hitler. 'I will control destiny! I will be master of my fate!'

And that is something that Bormann can understand. The desire to steer one's life through the dark and tumultuous waters that surround him. The need to constantly battle against all the storms and whirlpools of ill fortune that try to sink a man. He sits back and watches the Führer work on, and then asks if he'd like a cup of tea or something to drink. But Hitler ignores him, too busily moving scraps of paper back and forward.

Bormann boils himself some water, longing for a strong coffee, but all he finds in the cupboard are herbal teas. He decides to go without, and slips out of the room and goes back downstairs to the guest bedroom. He lies awake for some time, thinking about what the Führer has said and then he drifts off to sleep, wondering if it really might be possible to rewrite a person's past and his future. It is a pleasing thought, even if it is not more than a delusion. And he's been thinking a lot about delusions lately. For it has taken most of his life to understand that many visions are simply delusions wrapped in faith.

Bormann is sitting outside a small cell and trying to make out the figure who sits there in the semi-darkness. He is an aged balding man who has several newspapers spread out on a low desk before him.

Then the small man looks up and Bormann knows him. It is Adolf Eichmann, the former SS Obersturmbannführer who oversaw the concentration camps. He nods to Bormann and then goes back to his task. Bormann steps up closer to the bars, reluctant to touch them but wanting to see what Eichmann is doing. He is ripping lines out of the newspaper, then scrunching them up and eating them.

Bormann wants to ask him what he is doing, but Eichmann says, 'They won't let me have scissors.' His fingers leave rough awkward tears in the newspaper, like somebody has fought over the pages, stabbing out holes at random. But these are not random.

Bormann can see that Herr Eichmann is searching the newspapers for any mention of himself and ripping out any paragraphs that have his name in them. Purging his own name, as if that will somehow save him from his fate.

But he also sees that the more pages Eichmann turns, the more mentions of his name he finds. Some pages are more holes than paper, and Eichmann is struggling to feed more paper into his mouth. Already it is swollen and threatens to choke him. But he keeps ripping out sections with his name on them and squishing them into his mouth.

Bormann can hear his laboured breathing through his nose as he rolls his head about, his eyes filled with distress. Then he looks up at Bormann again and starts beckoning him to come closer. Still Bormann does not wish to touch the bars, but Eichmann is insistent. He gestures to his mouth and to Bormann, as if there is something vital that he has to tell him. Perhaps he knows about plans by the Israelis to kidnap him. He knows they are always searching for him. Eichmann would know what they are up to. Would be able to warn him.

'What do they know?' Bormann asks him.

But although Eichmann tries to speak, he can only make gurgling choking sounds.

'Tell me,' says Bormann. 'What do they know?'

But Eichmann is unable to tell him. He tries to rip some of the damp newspaper from his mouth, but there is too much of it. All balled up tightly. Choking him.

'Tell me,' says Bormann, convinced that it is vital to know what Eichmann is trying to tell him.

But just as he rips enough newspaper back out of his mouth to make a sound that is near human, a dark sack is cast over Eichmann's head and strong arms pull him away.

Now Bormann does grasp the bars, leans in close and stares into the cell, unable to see where Eichmann has gone. Unable to see the remains of the newspapers he had been ripping up. Unable to even see if he is outside a cell looking in, or inside a cell looking out.

Acht

All great movements are popular movements.

– Mein Kampf

Bormann is woken by the morning sun filling his little concrete block room with light, and he feels a thickness inside his mouth like he might have been chewing on newsprint himself. He also notes, as he sits up and moves about, that his head aches more than it ought to.

It takes a while for him to find his glasses and focus on his wristwatch. It is ten-thirty a.m. It takes him a moment longer to realise that he has not heard Hitler have his morning bowel movement. That is odd.

He sits up to find that he is still fully clothed, and he staggers up the stairs. He smells it as soon as he is halfway up. Gas! The upstairs of the house is thick with it. Bormann pushes the crook of his elbow against his mouth and nose and keeps climbing up the stairs. He hears his knee click a little and start to lose its strength, but continues. He emerges into the upper storey and the smell of gas is so thick it makes his head swim even worse.

He can hear the dangerous hiss coming from the kitchenette and stumbles towards it. He can see a kettle has boiled over and put out the gas fire, leaving the gas hissing. He quickly turns it off and throws open the window above it, starting to cough now.

Then he turns and calls out, '*Mein Führer*! Where are you?' And he sees Hitler slumped at the table, his face pale and drawn. '*Mein Führer*!' he says again, more loudly, but the old man does not respond. Bormann staggers across to him. He searches for a pulse but cannot find one. He listens for any sign of breathing, but cannot find any.

'*Mein Gott!*' he exclaims. He is as dead as his double in the bunker. As dead as Eva. Poor Eva. He feels tears welling in his eyes.

He has gassed Adolf Hitler! The Odessa organisation will cut his balls off and make him eat them if they find out. He drags the old man off the chair and over to the glass doors of the balcony. He is thankfully thin and light. He slides the doors open and feels the clean fresh air coming in. It tastes glorious. He grabs Hitler by one arm and drags him out onto the veranda. His head catches on the step and then bumps as he drags him clear.

'*Mein Führer!*' Bormann says once more, hoping that he will miraculously start breathing. But he does not. Bormann sinks to his knees beside the great man and takes a deep breath. Then he presses his lips to Hitler's and starts breathing steadily into his lungs. He has a fleeting thought of the homosexual Sturmabteilung leader Ernst Röhm, but pushes it aside. The old man's lips are dry and wrinkled. Like kissing prunes, he thinks. But he continues breathing his own life essence into the Führer. He turns his head and fills his lungs with clean air again, and once more presses his lips to the Führer's. He watches the way his stomach fills and he is trying to remember if that is a good sign or a bad one. Isn't the air meant to go into his lungs? Maybe he needs to tilt his head back a little more. He repositions the Führer's head and takes another breath of air and presses his lips to Hitler's. This time his lungs rise more than his stomach. He repeats the process several times and then suddenly he feels the Führer stir beneath his hands.

He cradles his head in his lap as he coughs and splutters. Hitler vomits up a small amount of orange liquid onto Bormann and then is breathing. Is moving. His arms are flapping around him, trying to disentangle himself from his secretary's grasp.

It takes Hitler a few moments to recover and the first thing he says is, 'Why are you embracing me? Let me go! You have vomited on yourself.'

'*Mein Führer!*' says Bormann and struggles to climb to his feet, then helps Hitler to his feet too. Then he snaps to attention and says, 'I wish to report that the gas was on in the house and you had succumbed to it. I saved your life. I…I…I turned off the gas and dragged you out here.' He can't bring himself to say more. Is suddenly short of breath. Feels his heart racing in his old chest.

'What do you mean, the gas was on?' Hitler asks him.

And Bormann feels he himself is going to faint now. Closes his eyes tightly and tries to will his heart to slow just a little. 'The gas. It appeared that you – that someone – had left the kettle on and it had boiled over and put out the gas fire. I have read of such things happening, though I can't remember where.'

'Are you suggesting?' asks Hitler, 'that somebody tried to kill me?'

And Bormann blinks rapidly and then says, 'Perhaps we need to undertake a full investigation…'

'Do you think it's Mossad?' asks the Führer quickly. 'Do you think that they have found us?'

And for a moment Bormann is back in his dream. In his worst nightmare. He shakes it away and says, 'I think…well, no. I don't believe so.'

'Then perhaps it's Von Stauffenberg?' suggests Hitler.

'You had him executed for the bomb plot on your life,' says Bormann.

'Ah yes. I had forgotten. Then who do you think it was?'

'I am unable to say,' says Bormann.

'It is most distressing,' says Hitler, and settles onto one of the deckchairs. 'If we had had a chance to have our fortunes told by rune stones, we could have prevented it altogether.' Then he looks up at Bormann closely. But Bormann is unwilling to meet his eyes. 'Perhaps it was the local council?' the Führer asks. 'It shows they are desperate. But they are going to have to try much harder than this if they wish to silence me. I have survived so many assassination attempts that I have developed a sixth sense, you know.'

'My Führer never fails to impress me,' says Bormann.

'Did you also know that the Gestapo counted over twenty-five attempts on my life? Many I only avoided by changing my schedule at the last moment?'

'Yes. I knew,' says Bormann. There were so many bomb attempts, and each caused the Führer to isolate himself from the world a little more.

The two men sit in silence a moment and then Hitler says, 'The Allies sent assassins and spies, and they tried to kill me by bombing the whole city of Berlin. But it was those closest to me who caused me the most pain. Albert Speer, General Rommel, Ernst Röhm!'

Bormann coughs and Hitler wipes some of the orange muck off his lips.

'Do you know how many people died in my place?' he asks Bormann.

Bormann, not sure how to answer, shakes his head.

'It was twelve people,' says Hitler. 'Eight died in the bomb blast at the Bürgerbräukeller in Munich in 1939, and four more died in the bomb blast at the Wolf's Lair in 1944.'

'Of course,' says Bormann, although he has a memory of the last days in the bunker when Generals Burgdorf and Krebs accused him of causing the death of millions of civilians, when they were trying to convince him not to flood the underground metro to prevent the Russians using the tunnels to advance through the city, as they were filled with civilians hiding from the fighting. General Burgdorf accused him of murdering them all. Told him the numbers of dead were so high that one human being could never envisage that many bodies.

'Yes, twelve people,' Hitler says solemnly. A number clearly more easy to envisage.

'Their sacrifices were not in vain,' says Bormann. General Burgdorf was a defeatist; he killed himself at the end.

'They think perhaps their vain attempts on my life fill me with fear,' says Hitler, going off on a new tangent, 'but they only affirm my resolve. They are spineless cowards. They shall feel my vengeance.' He coughs up some more carrot mush. 'Do you remember when the partisans assassinated Reynard Heydrich?' he asks. 'We had every single man in the Czech village of Lidice killed in reprisal.' He sighs. 'I miss those days, you know.'

'Of course, *mein Führer*,' says Bormann, glad to have dodged a metaphorical bullet himself. 'Let me help you inside.'

And Hitler looks at his watch. 'Yes. I must go to the toilet and have a bowel movement,' he says. 'I am late.'

Uncle's house smells like our house did the time the ambulance came and took Mummy to hospital. When they let her home again, she kept saying, 'Anyone can make a mistake in life.' And she laughed. It must have been another joke. She slept in my room for a whole week after that and said I didn't need to go to school because she was feeling under the weather.

She is under the weather again this morning, but says that I can go and visit Uncle, but not to be a nuisance. When I get to Uncle's house, 269 steps away, and see him and his friend out on the veranda and smell the house, I ask if the ambulance is going to come and take them away, and if so, then they must insist that it was an accident, even if the police come and try to tell them it wasn't.

Uncle's friend asks me what on earth I am talking about, but Uncle shushes him. Because the house smells so bad on the inside, we all sit out on the veranda looking out at the ocean. It is very blue today. One day, I think, I will count all the different blues that the ocean can be.

There is a ship far out at sea and the two men watch it as if might be bringing them a present that they have really, really been wanting for a long time. But the ship just continues on its way and sails past. Uncle showed me how you could tell how far out at sea a ship was by taking angle readings at two different places on land and then marking those on a map. I really like the idea of that, and have been thinking about all the different things you could measure with a map. I told Mummy, but she said maps couldn't figure out any of the things that really mattered. She said there were no maps for parenthood or for happiness, though I think life would be a lot easier if there were.

And then Uncle's friend says, 'Do you ever worry that if you disappeared one day, it would take others a very long time to even realise it?'

'Why would I disappear?' Uncle asks him.

'For too many reasons,' his friend says.

The two men sit there in silence for what seems like a very long time, but when I check my watch, it is only five and half minutes.

Then Uncle says, 'Come. We will go for a walk and clear all these melancholic cobwebs out of our heads.'

Neun

Never forget that the most sacred right on this earth is man's
right to have the earth to till with his own hands, the most
sacred sacrifice the blood that a man sheds for this earth…

– Mein Kampf

While the house airs, Hitler, Bormann and Adam walk down the hill
to the beach. The wind blows to the south today and has a tang of
bushland in it. They walk along the sands in silent contemplation. It is
a blustery day and low clouds march past them like a parade of ghosts.
The ocean throws up a motley-coloured dark foam onto the shore.
Flotsam and driftwood are piled up at the high tide mark. Bormann
pauses and looks down at the remains of a dead seagull at his feet. Its
feathers are spiky and sea-logged. The one eye he can see has a thick
film of death over it. Even Hitler stops to look at it. Adam is busy
trying to find seashells that are an exact match of each other.

Bormann kicks sand over the bird, as if to accord it something of
a burial.

Hitler lifts his head and looks out across the ocean. 'I came down
here after the British sank the Argentinian cruiser the *General Belgrano*,'
he says. 'It was a day just like this.'

Bormann looks down at the dead seagull again and imagines that
somewhere in Argentina there might be people standing on a beach,
still waiting for the bodies of the dead sailors to wash up on the shore.
Over 300 men went down when the British torpedoed the ship, because
it had sailed into their so-called exclusion zone. That was the point the
war became real. Exceeded what the military might call a 'skirmish'.
The British and the allies hooted and crowed, while the Argentinians

and their allies wept in outrage. Bormann was contemptuous of them both. It was a war, for God's sake. You didn't go to war and then act surprised by such things.

'Do you know the history of Eden?' Hitler asks Bormann suddenly.

'Only what I've read in the Bible,' Bormann replies.

'The town was built as a whaling station,' Hitler says. 'It is largely fishing now, though, and they have two memorials to the dead further up along the bay here. The first is a memorial to those who served and died in the war, like all these small towns have, but the other is a memorial to those who have died at sea. It is a long wall with plaques for the dead.'

They walk on a little way.

'One commemorates those who died battling nature and the other commemorates those who died battling the nature of men,' Hitler says. Then he looks around for Adam, who is still engrossed in seashells.

Hitler looks back out to sea and says, 'I have often wondered how they commemorate the war dead in the Fatherland these days.'

But Bormann cannot tell him. He has never returned to Germany either since their long years of exile.

'They used to hunt whales out there,' Hitler says and he points at the choppy ocean. 'The amazing thing is, though, that killer whales used to help the men. When a whale would swim past, the killer whales would act like a wolf pack and herd it towards shore. One of the killer whales would even swim into the whaling station and splash the water to alert the men there. They'd jump in their boat and the killer whale would lead them out to the whale, which was being harried by the rest of the pack.'

Bormann looks incredulous.

'It's true,' says Hitler. 'The men would kill the whale and let the killer whales eat the lips and tongue. The men would tow the rest back to shore. They'd drag the carcasses up onto the beach on the other side of the bay here, and cut the skin off until the water would run red with blood. They say the stench was so strong it drew scavenger birds and sharks from miles around.' He stares out into the emptiness for some time and then asks, 'Can you imagine it?'

Bormann has never seen a whale, and cannot picture one being cut apart, its skin peeled off its hulk and blood running out. But he's seen U-boats split apart from enemy fire. He's seen the aftermath of invasion beaches where bodies littered the sands, staining the water red. So he says, 'Yes, I can picture it.'

They walk on in silence for some distance and then Hitler says, 'Talking of the Bible, did you know they tell a story here about a fisherman who was swallowed by a whale and was then cut out of it, alive?'

'How was it possible?' asks Bormann.

'He was lost from a fishing boat and the whale swallowed him whole. The whale was then caught, the next day, and when they dragged it up on the beach to cut it open, they found the fisherman inside. He was unconscious, but still alive. They revived him.'

'Amazing,' says Bormann.

'They say his skin had been bleached white from the stomach acids inside the whale and all his hair was gone.'

They weave around a wave that sweeps up closer to them, pushing up seaweed and dirty foam.

'It was like he was reborn, do you see?' says Hitler.

Bormann wonders if the Führer is talking about himself and his return from death, so he says, 'Of course.' Then, 'What became of him?'

'He lived for many years afterwards, but that's incidental to the miracle of being reborn.'

Bormann nods. 'Of course.'

And they walk on, their footsteps weaving a parallel line along the shoreline, the mark of their path and contemplation.

Soon they reach the end of the beach, where a stream blocks their way. The two men turn round and Bormann can see the distant figure of the boy, still crouched over, examining shells. Definitely something a little odd about the boy, he thinks. But clearly harmless enough.

Then he notes that the waves have erased one set of footsteps at several points along the beach where they have come, as if only one of them had actually been there. And that fills him with a sense of melancholy, as he thinks which of them will prove to be the last man walking.

Back at the far end of the beach on their return walk, Hitler indicates a small graveyard, right on the ocean front. 'It is a strange thing,' the Führer says, 'that many of the small towns along the coast here built their graveyards facing the sea. Often the best land in town.'

'We are thinking too much of death today,' Bormann says.

'Perhaps,' says Hitler and he leads Bormann into the graveyard. 'The land is divided up by religions,' he tells Bormann. 'See, here is the Church of England section. Here is the Catholic section.'

Bormann walks around the old gravestones, reading the inscriptions. The oldest stones, closest to the ocean, have been worn down by the elements and are difficult to read. Bormann can make out bits of words and a few of the dates of death. 1889. 1890. A row back, the stones are easier to read. Some have a few short lines about the person's life carved into them. Where the person had been born and what they had done in their life. Who they had married and where and how many children they had.

Bormann sees that often the children have been buried either side of their parents. The tombstones are nothing like the elaborate marble stones he has seen in German cemeteries, but neither are they like the paupers' graves he has seen in South America.

Scattered throughout the graveyard are simple white concrete crosses like you might see in a military graveyard, with the simple word 'Unknown' painted on them with black paint. He stands in front of one and stares at it. He has seen hundreds of these types of crosses across Europe where unidentified corpses have been buried.

But Hitler steps up beside him and says, 'They are not unknown bodies. They are unknown corpses.'

'What is the difference?' Bormann asks.

'When they have dug grave sites here to bury people, they have often found unmarked graves with the remains of people in them. So they have reburied them. These crosses mark their locations.'

Bormann finds that somehow shocking. He is not surprised to think that a person could be killed and nobody know who they were, but that a person who once had a family and friends and colleagues could die but their grave be lost – that is quite beyond his conception.

As he walks among the graves, he sees that many of those who died more recently have a photo of the deceased sealed into the tombstone. A small window into the character of the person interred below. He wonders if, when he is finally buried, what photograph of him they might choose to place on his grave. A photo of him as a younger man, he suspects, simply because he has been so careful to avoid having his photo taken in the last thirty-five years.

He walks along the roads reading the names there. Woods. Armstrong. Davidson. Egan.

'This is a strange town, this Eden,' says Hitler. 'Almost every other small town has a special marker in the cemetery for those killed in the war, but here they are simply buried amongst their family members.'

He points at one tombstone with a soldier's military symbol on it. Bormann notes that the man did not actually die in the war, but years later.

'There is something else you should see, over here,' says Hitler, and he leads Bormann down the far right corner of the cemetery.

The graves look the same as any other, but Bormann reads the names. Herman. Switzer. Brandt. And even Eichmann! German names, here in Eden. He notes that a married couple with the surname Eichmann are buried together, having died only in the last few years, and they were roughly the same age as him. Their given names on the tombstone are 'Noel' and 'Nelly', marked in quote marks to show they are not their actual names, but the names they were known by.

'Many Germans found it advantageous to change their family names during the two world wars, but in this case they only appear to have changed their first names, not their family names. I wonder why?'

And Bormann has no answer. Perhaps once they were dead it didn't matter what their surnames were. He thinks that he would much prefer to have Bormann on his tombstone than Lukas.

'Have you seen enough?' asks Hitler.

'I have seen enough death to last many lifetimes,' he says. 'But now I need to pee again.'

Uncle has taken us for a walk through the graveyard. I don't know why tombstones only have a person's name and date of birth and death on them, and nothing else. The dates are good because you can go around and do sums at each tombstone, figuring out how old they were. Some of the older tombstones don't have the full birth details, which is annoying. They should put those tombstones in their own area of the cemetery, so those people who get upset when they can't do the sums on them don't need to see them. They should also put more information on the stones, like how good a person was at maths, and what their favourite colours were.

My mother would put different details on them, though. When we've walked down to the beach past the graveyard, she has stopped at some of the newer tombstones and said, 'He was an adulterer. It doesn't say that there!' or 'He committed suicide. Why don't they say that?' Or 'He was an alko. Drank himself to death. They should say that there too.'

Mummy says that she doesn't want anyone to just sum up her life in a name and dates. She says she wants a poem or something, and that I should write something for her. I don't like poetry though. It has too many perhapses. I'd rather writes sums for her. Long and complicated sums that all ended up neatly in the end. I told her that and she said she'd rather a poem. That caused me a lot of concerns, and I worried that she would need to have her tombstone moved into the annoying section of the graveyard. But then I thought of an idea. I could use a code, whereby each letter was the number of its place in the alphabet, and I could invent a poem that was also a sum. So her name

Eve Gardiner would be 5 22 5 + 7 1 18 4 9 14 5 18. And going back the other way, from numbers to letters, using the code, her birthday would be ACSFA, which isn't a real word, but if I move the letters and numbers forward or backwards it makes new words, like MOERM or IYLG. They're not real words either, but I'm sure if I do enough work on this code I can come up with real words to make into a poem.

I haven't told her this idea yet. Maybe I'll keep it a secret until I've got it worked out. I told Uncle about it, though, and he told me that secret codes can be very important and that he had hundreds of men and women working for him to keep all his messages secret. His birthday as a word is TDAIDE. If I had hundreds of men and women helping me, I'm sure we could work out how to do a poem that was also a sum. Working alone, it might take me many years, I think, but that's okay, because I want Mummy to live for many, many more years.

I asked Uncle if he and his friend use codes to talk to each other, and he said, 'It is the only safe way to talk to each other.' Which explains why I don't really understand many of the things they are saying.

Then I asked him what he would like written on his tombstone and he went very quiet for a long time, before he said, 'I have no intention of dying. I have too many important things still to do.'

My mummy complains about all the things she has to do, but I'll tell her there's no need to worry about them now as they are good for her. I wonder what Uncle's friend's birthday is, and what word it would make? I asked him, but he said that was impolite to ask. So I made up a birthday for him. 14 July 1825, which when you put a 1 at the front makes the word ANGRY, which shows my poem code idea can work.

Zehn

Any alliance whose purpose is not the intention
to wage war is senseless and useless.

– *Mein Kampf*

They go back to the newsagent on their return walk and Hitler looks down his nose with contempt at the few surfie lads hanging about on the main street. 'If we were in England, these would be skinheads,' he says. 'Abusing us for being foreigners in their land. Threatening us with violence. Waving the British flag around like it was a shield.'

They step past the surfies into the shop.

'Youth here are disappointing. They have no mettle,' Hitler says. He takes a copy of the *Daily Mirror* and says, 'Good morning, Mrs Dubrovic.'

Adam goes to look at the *Phantom* comics.

'Good morning, Mr Schicklgruber,' she says.

'Any sign of your dog?' Bormann asks, trying to sound a little optimistic.

'No,' she says sadly. Then to Hitler, 'I'm sure you were right about that Asian butcher. He's selling meat far too cheaply for it to be anything but dog.'

Hitler tut-tuts.

'They don't belong in our country,' she says. 'They should all be sent back where they came from.'

'That's the spirit,' says Hitler.

'I'd like to smash his windows and burn his shop down,' she says.

'Yes!' says Hitler.

'I'd teach him a lesson!'

'I know you would,' he says.

'I've rung the council,' she says in a whisper. 'They'll see to him. Probably run him out of town.'

'Bravo!' Hitler says.

'Do you know what I think, personally,' she says, leaning closer over the counter.

'Tell me,' says Hitler.

'I think they're going to over-run the country if we don't stop them. Where will we be in fifty years otherwise? We won't have a single dog left in the country. I think we need to see an end to it before they see an end to us.'

And Hitler leans in close to her and says, 'Those are my own thoughts and my own words exactly.'

She straightens up and adjusts her cardigan and says, 'I didn't used to think that way, but you've made me see things differently.'

'I'm gratified to hear it,' says Hitler. 'You give me confidence in the future of the nation.'

Then he leads Bormann and Adam back outside, past the surfer boys, and the two old men sit on a bench while Adam sits on the gutter's edge and counts patterns of stones in the bitumen.

Hitler consults his horoscope. 'I must beware of making hasty decisions,' he says. 'Best colour black and best number 9. Hmm.' He ponders that for some time and then turns the newspaper to the front pages.

'What is the news on the Falklands war?' Bormann asks him.

Hitler reads on for a moment and then says, 'It is all propaganda today. It says the British troops have taken the mountains overlooking Port Stanley after fierce fighting. It lists the mountains as Mount Longdon, Mount Harriet and Two Sisters. It says fatalities are estimated at about twenty-five on the British side and about a hundred on the Argentinian side.' He reads on a bit more, turning to the inside pages.

Bormann peers over to get a glimpse at the page three girl. Not quite Victoria Principal, he thinks, but not too bad.

'It also says the British are now poised to take Port Stanley but expect fierce resistance from the Argentinians and are worried about the Falklands civilians being caught in the crossfire. There is even concern that the Argentinians will use them as hostages.' He reads some more in silence. 'And listen to this,' he says. 'A British destroyer has been badly damaged by a land-based Exocet missile. Numbers of casualties have not been released yet but are expected to be high. That's giving the British a taste of what's to come. The Argentinians are going to let them come in close and them cut them down at the gates of the city. Just as we did to the Russians in Berlin. Over-confidence is a great mistake in war,' he cautions.

Bormann can only agree with him, and presumes Hitler is now talking about the re-enactments he has staged in his basement.

'The British will advance on the capital, thinking they have overcome all resistance, and then General Wenk's 12th Army with link up with Obergruppenführer Steiner's 9th Army, and encircle them from behind and crush them,' he says.

'Perhaps we should be getting home now,' says Bormann. 'You should be careful not to over-exert yourself, *Mein Führer.*'

'I might be ninety-three,' Hitler says, 'but I tell you that I have the constitution of an eighty-three-year-old!'

Bormann, who will turn eighty-two in a few weeks, and is quite exhausted from the exertions of the morning, says, 'I can only hope that I will be as healthy as the Führer when I am your age.'

'Come then,' Hitler says. 'Let us return to the Eagle's Lair.'

It is a long slow walk back up the hill and when the two old Nazis reach Hitler's house, they find a car in the driveway waiting for them.

'The enemy are at the gates,' says the Führer as a man climbs out of the car.

'Mr Schicklgruber,' he says, walking across with his hand held out.

Hitler just stares at the man's hand until he slowly withdraws it.

'Councillor Michael Wright,' he says.

Bormann sees that the man is in his early fifties, has dark hair and small Christ-like beard, and in his pale green suit, which no longer fits his spreading paunch, he looks far too much like a lawyer for his tastes.

'May I come in?' he asks.

'We are having the house fumigated,' says Hitler. 'There are too many vermin around.'

'Oh,' the councillor says. 'Nothing too serious, I hope?'

'Nothing some minor extermination won't deal with,' Hitler says coolly.

'Have you called my brother-in-law, Rick the Flick Man? You've probably seen his ads around town. He's a whiz at extermination.'

'I have sufficient experience myself,' Hitler says.

'Well, that's fine then.' He rocks back and forward on his heels a moment and says, 'So. The reason I've come is to try and sort out this situation we have. I thought we might be able to have a little chat and see if we can't find some solution.'

'The simplest solution is to leave things be,' says Hitler.

'Well, that's just not possible, I'm afraid. Mr Dikowski has lodged an official complaint and the council surveyor has confirmed that you've breached the property line.'

'Perhaps you should simply redraw the property line,' says Martin Bormann.

Councillor Wright turns to him and says, 'I'm sorry, we haven't been introduced,' and he holds out his hand for him to shake.

Bormann just stares at it.

'This is my guest, Mr...um...'

'Lukas. Josef Lukas,' says Bormann.

'Pleased to meet you,' the councillor says. 'We always welcome visitors to our town.' Then, 'Perhaps you could be of some assistance in helping Mr Schicklgruber see some sense here. I presume you're an old friend of his?'

'He's actually the president of Hungary, here on an incognito visit,' says Hitler.

Councillor Wright raises his eyebrows, looking a little dubious. 'Really?' he asks.

And now Martin Bormann does take his hand and shakes it heartily and he says in a soft voice, 'We'd appreciate it if you'd keep it to yourself, though. The Department of Foreign Affairs thinks I'm in Sydney for a few days of business meetings. The bureaucrats get awfully wound up if they think they've lost a president. We'd have ASIO agents and government officials crawling all over the town if they knew I was here.'

'Uh, of course,' says Councillor Wright. 'I understand. Discretion is my middle name.'

'That was an odd choice of your parents,' says Bormann.

'Um, no, it's not my real name. It's just an expression.'

'Ah. An idiom,' says Bormann. 'I must remember that.'

'Yes. Quite,' says Councillor Wright, a little flustered now. And he tries to steer the conversation back to the property line dispute. 'We discussed this issue at the council meeting last night and it was decided that we should try to solve things through mediation before taking further action.'

'Mediation?' asks Bormann. 'What is this? It is not a word I am familiar with.'

'Well, it's when two parties come together, with a mediator or a facilitator, and we try and work out a compromise that is acceptable to both parties.'

'I don't believe we have such a word in Hungarian,' says Bormann.

'Then what do you do in the case of disputes like this one?' asks the councillor.

'The parties come together and they must work out a solution between themselves.'

'Well, I can see some benefit in that…'

'With knives,' says Bormann.

Now the councillor starts to look a little dubious again.

'But only flesh wounds are permitted,' says Hitler. 'It is an old custom that dates back hundreds of years and you know how difficult it is to change old customs in Europe.'

'Well, that's an interesting point to raise,' the councillor says, 'because this issue comes down to customs too. It's really about fitting into our community as we have a certain way of doing things here in Eden and we'd like to think that all members of the community, whether they're new arrivals or long-established families, would fit in with the way the community does things.'

Hitler and Bormann say nothing but just stare at the councillor, who starts to stammer a little as he tries to clarify what he is saying, without causing insult.

'It's something the whole council agree to, and we even considered drafting a statement of accord that would say, in words yet to be agreed on, that if people want to live in our community then they need to conform to a certain set of values that are inherent in our community. Do you see what I'm saying?'

'Are you saying that Mr Dikowski does not belong here because he is causing conflict?' says Hitler.

'Well, no. No I'm not. And perhaps I'm not being clear enough in this, but it is the feeling of council that it's not Mr Dikowski who is the cause of the conflict here. He's not the one who is threatening council workers with violence, and he's not the one who is threatening to march on the council chambers. He has always been willing to take part in mediation.'

'I am happy to take part in mediation,' says Hitler suddenly and Councillor Wright smiles broadly.

'Well, that's splendid. That's wonderful to hear.'

'Should we put a restriction on the knife size?'

Councillor Wright rubs the bridge of his nose between his eyes as if he can feel a sudden headache coming on.

'No. No. No,' he says. 'We're talking about sitting down and talking this out.'

'To what benefit?'

'Well, to find a solution that is amenable to both parties.'

'But I only have one position that is amenable to me – that Mr Dikowski withdraw his complaint and that you allow me to leave my shed where it is.'

Councillor Wright takes a deep breath and says, 'I'm sorry to say that we can't allow that. Council has already decided that if you do not comply with council orders to move your shed back across to your side of the property line, we will come in and forcibly move it.'

'How will you do that?' Hitler asks.

'Well, to be blunt, with a bulldozer. We will push it back across to your side of the property line.'

Hitler stares at the councillor for some long moments and then says, in a soft voice, 'That sounds to me like a declaration of war.'

'That's a very strong word,' says the councillor, holding up his hands. 'Far too strong for the situation.'

'The Hungarian press is always very interested in stories like this,' Bormann says. 'And I hope nobody tells the Australian newspapers and television that I am here or it will be in all the local media too.'

Councillor Wright rubs the bridge of his nose again. 'Well, that wouldn't help anybody,' he says.

'It might help us,' Hitler says. 'Pensioner bullied by council. I think it would be a very popular story.'

'Now there's no need to make threats,' the councillor says.

'I never make threats,' says Hitler. 'Only statements of fact.'

'There is an idiom in Hungarian,' says Bormann, 'we call *Anschlüss*.'

'What does that mean?' the councillor asks.

'Total mediation,' says Bormann.

'What will we do?' Bormann asks, showing a little more concern and panic than he had shown in front of the councillor, after Mr Wright has driven off.

Adam, who made himself scarce during the councillor's visit, suddenly appears beside Hitler and says, 'He's such an *Arschloch*.'

Now Hitler has to feign surprise. 'I can't image where he learned that,' he says, and then changes the subject. 'Come. We shall prepare lunch and then we shall prepare to repel the invaders.'

'You have defences?' Bormann asks him.

'Does the Pope defecate in the woods?' Hitler asks him.

'I'm sorry, what?'

'It is an idiom,' says Hitler. 'I hear people using it in town.'

'*Ach* so,' says Bormann. Then, 'What does it mean?'

'Like most Australian idioms, it means whatever you want it to mean.'

Bormann frowns a little, trying to understand it.

'Like the word shit,' says Hitler. 'The Australians have good shit and they have bad shit and they are full of shit and they couldn't give a shit and they say people shit them, and they say things are shit hot, and they even have Holy Shit!'

'*Scheisser*,' says Adam.

Hitler looks at him and frowns. 'He's very quick with languages,' he says.

'Which must relate to the Pope defecating in the woods,' says Bormann.

'I believe so,' says Hitler.

'I think I understand now,' says Bormann, although clearly he does not.

'Good,' says Hitler. 'For lunch, let me offer you a choice of mashed vegetables, mostly carrot, or mashed vegetables, mostly greens.'

'You choose,' says Bormann, knowing that whatever choice he makes it will be no better than the other. Bad shit.

'Turn on the gas for me then,' says Hitler. 'If you dare…'

After their meal, served out on the balcony overlooking the ocean, Bormann feels he would like nothing more than to have a lie down and sleep for an hour or two. He is quite done in with the day so far.

But Hitler seems to be getting more energy as the day progresses. 'Come,' he says, leaving Adam at the table drawing maps, and kicks Bormann's leg before leading him down to the front yard. 'The first line of defences,' he says, pointing at a rotary sprinkler in the middle of the front lawn. 'What do you see?'

'Um – a water sprinkler,' says Bormann.

'Aha,' says Hitler. 'That's the successful art of deception. And why do you suppose the grass all around it is dead?'

'I can only speculate that it does not work.'

'Oh yes, it works, but it does not spray water.'

Bormann bends down on aged legs and carefully sniffs around the sprinkler. 'Petrol!' he says.

'I call this defence the wall of flames,' says Hitler.

Bormann is shocked. 'You would ignite petrol onto the council workers?'

'Of course,' says Hitler. 'Do you know how hard it is to fire a rifle at our age? The kickback leaves bruises that takes months to heal.'

Bormann is unable to disagree. The last time he was offered a rifle to fire, several years ago at a neo-Nazi training camp in South Africa, it felt so heavy he could not even hold it steady enough to aim.'

'Come,' says Hitler. 'Now we look at our second line of defences.' And he leads Bormann towards the outside stairs they have just descended. 'What do you see?' Hitler asks.

Bormann looks around carefully. There is a faded concrete pelican and a concrete Aboriginal, standing with one foot raised against the other leg's knee. 'I am not sure what I see,' Bormann says. 'Only some statues.'

'Again, the art of deception and camouflage,' Hitler says. 'The statues are both hollowed out and filled with explosives.'

'Brilliant,' says Bormann.

'Now, the third line of defences,' says Hitler and he leads Bormann up the side driveway to the shed. 'Sooner or later they will try and enter the shed, yes?'

'I believe so,' says Bormann.

'And what will they find?'

Bormann shakes his head. Hitler presses his body against the garage door and tries to lift it. It shakes but does not yield. Bormann takes hold of the handle too and together the two old warriors get it open.

'What do you see?' asks Hitler.

There is an old Volkswagen, even older and more decrepit than the one that the police confiscated.

'I see a Volkswagen, which is obviously another clever super-weapon,' says Bormann.

'Yes,' says Hitler. 'It is a car bomb. I got the idea from the car bombs they explode in Beirut. I have filled the car with shrapnel and all I need do is ignite the petrol in its fuel tank.'

'A masterstroke,' says Bormann.

'Aha,' says Hitler. 'Not quite. The next line of defence is my masterstroke. Come,' and he leads Bormann further into the crowded shed.

They have to climb over an old ride-on mower and some boxes until they come to what looks like the remains of a television set that has been cannibalised and hooked up to a small satellite dish and a microwave covered with wires.

'What is it?' asks Bormann.

'A death ray!' says Hitler grandly.

Bormann is awed.

'Some of Himmler's scientists were working on it towards the end of the war.'

'How does it work?' Bormann asks.

'It focuses microwaves into a concentrated beam that destabilises a person's nervous system, leaving them twitching and shaking, unable to function.'

Bormann watches the way the Führer's own body twitches and shakes as he says it, but all he himself says is, 'If only we'd had such a weapon during the war!'

'Exactly!' says Hitler. 'It is all Himmler's fault of course, always promising me super-weapons that never arrived or failed to work properly. Invisible suits. Jet planes. Ultrasonic noise rays that could disable a tank. Even the atom bomb! He promised me them all, but did I ever see them? No. Now the Allies have them all in their hands.' Hitler draws himself up and says, proudly, 'This time we will vanquish the enemy as we should have done in Berlin.'

And Bormann finds that the only words that come to him, despite his concerns, are 'I am filled with admiration for your military genius.'

And Hitler nods as if there was nothing other that he expected Bormann to say.

Uncle is showing his friend around our secret traps. He is the only person Uncle has ever shown them to. Besides me of course. I hope he is going to set them off. I have been waiting to see them for a long time. Uncle says it will be like a great fireworks show, and that I should not be afraid of all the noise and fire. He says it can be very scary at first, but then you get used to it very quickly.

Mummy takes me to see fireworks when there is a carnival in town, and of course on fireworks night everyone is letting off bungers and sky rockets. Two boys put bungers in Uncle's letter box last year and blew it to pieces. They tied lots of bungers together and wrapped all their wicks so they'd all blow up at once. The lid went flying off the letter box, and that's what Uncle did: he lost his lid too. He was furious. He did the lying down and rolling around on the carpet thing he sometimes does, and then when he got up again he was very calm and he asked me if I knew which boys had done this to him. I told him that I was pretty certain because two boys had been caught putting bungers in the exhaust pipe of the police car. Uncle then asked me if I would show him where they lived and meet him after dinner that night. I asked him if there would be any fireworks involved, and he said there definitely would be.

So after dark we crept down to Billy Penfold's house and when we go there Uncle pulled a really funny-looking stick out of his pocket. It had a small metal tin on one end.

'What is that?' I asked him.

'It's called a potato masher,' he said.

But I don't think that was true, because it was a really strong firework. He unscrewed a little metal piece at the bottom of the stick and a little string dropped out. He pulled the string and dropped the masher into the Penfold's brick letter box and then said, 'Run!'

We ran. We really, really ran, and hadn't gone too far when there was the loudest bang I had ever heard. It hurt my ears. I stopped to look back, and you wouldn't have believed that bungers or anything could damage a brick letter box, but this had even blown all the bricks out of the fence and smashed a few windows. There was smoke everywhere and it was amazing. Then Uncle grabbed my arm and pulled me quickly away. Lights were coming on all up the street as people opened their doors to see what had happened.

'Will we go to Johno McDonald's place now?' I asked Uncle.

Johno's place didn't have a brick letter box so the masher firework would be sure to make an even bigger amount of damage at his place.

'Not tonight,' Uncle said. 'Another night, perhaps.'

But we never did. Perhapses are like that. It was like he'd forgotten about it. I reminded him once about it, but he said there were more important things to do. So I helped him. The police had been around trying to find out who had blown apart the Penfold's letter box and the kids at school said somebody had used so many bungers that they'd made a bomb. So I left a note in the police station mailbox saying that Johno McDonald did it.

Then the police visited Johno and Billy's places both and the kids at school reckoned that if the police could prove anything they might go to jail. But they were too young for jail, others said. But nothing happened in the end, except the Penfolds rebuilt their letter box and fixed all their broken windows.

Anyway I don't think I'd be scared if Uncle exploded some of his secret traps. I think it would it would be more exciting than seeing Billy Penfold's letter box get blown sky high. Especially if Michael Wright is in the driveway at the time. That'd be really something to see. I have imagined it many times. Shooting fire at him. Blowing up bombs at him.

I'll tell Uncle that he's not to let off his secret traps if I'm not here to see them.

Elf

Germany will either be a world power or will not be at all.

– Mein Kampf

The two old men sit on the veranda throughout the afternoon, watching the grey clouds moving up the coast. Watching container ships go past far out at sea. Watching seagulls glide on the breeze. Watching trucks come and go along the highway. Watching young hoons with P-plates drive their cars noisily up and down in front of the shops. Watching for the convoy of council vehicles that never arrives.

Hitler is nursing an old service Luger that looks, to Bormann's aged eyes, a little rusted and decrepit and probably more dangerous to the user than the person it might be pointed at. And sitting there, he also wonders if the Führer has ever fired a gun at a man. He served in the First World War, of course, but much of that fighting was done hiding in the trenches. As far as Bormann knows, the only man he has ever shot up close was the time he fired a bullet into the head of his drugged double in the bunker. That must have been an unsettling experience, he thinks. But so much of those last days was unsettling.

Bormann then also wonders if bullets have use-by dates after which they become less effective. He'd read somewhere, though he couldn't remember where any more, somebody saying that Simon Wiesenthal and the other Nazi hunters should call off their fruitless searching as any old Nazis had surely passed their use-by dates. He had agreed with the sentiment at the time, but now, sitting here on the veranda of Hitler's house, waiting for the enemy to attack, he knows how wrong it was. The Führer will never have a use-by date.

'Do you know,' Hitler says, 'this always reminds me of looking out over the valley from my chalet at the Berghof. It had a view not unlike this.' And he waves his hand out over the vista before them.

Bormann, who has been to the Führer's Bavarian retreat many times, says, 'Yes, it does.'

'Except for the ocean perhaps,' says Hitler.

'Of course,' says Bormann.

'And the eucalypt trees,' says Hitler.

'Naturally,' says Bormann.

'And the small township here.'

'Yes.'

'But otherwise, not unlike this at all.'

Bormann is running out of fatuous statements of agreement, something he could never have imagined in his youth, when finally Hitler says, 'They won't be coming today.'

'Are you sure?'

'I'm positive. It is after four o'clock. All the council workers will be at the pub by four-thirty, drinking.' He shakes his head sadly. 'They can't even organise to invade an old man's property on time.' He shakes his head again and says, 'I have always been disappointed by my enemies, did you know?'

Bormann finds he still has at least one fatuous statement of agreement in him, and says, 'It does not surprise me to hear it, as you were always the superior of any of them.'

Hitler nods and then starts counting off on his fingers. 'Stalin was nothing but a thug. Churchill was a chain-smoking alcoholic. Truman was a cripple. Patton was a megalomaniac who only succeeded because of the sheer number of tanks he commanded. And Montgomery had the imagination of a man with no dress sense.'

Bormann doesn't ask about General Eisenhower or President Roosevelt.

Then Hitler says, 'Let us go inside and open a bottle of carrot juice to keep away the evening's chill.'

And Bormann, dreading the way he is going to feel in the morning, follows his leader as he knows he will do until he reaches his own rapidly approaching use-by date.

Half a bottle later, Hitler is building up a head of steam exposing the political problems in Australia that they won't encounter when they relocate to South America.

'The prime minister of this country has no idea how to lead this country,' he says. 'This Mr Fraser tries, yes, he tries, but he is not disciplined enough. Not strict enough. Let me tell you what he should do. Firstly he should introduce conscription. Put all men into the army to give them some moral backbone and national pride. After that, he should address the issue of refugees. Have you seen the stories about these boat people landing in the north? They charter a boat in Vietnam, which of course only the rich can do, and head south to Australia, and as soon as they reach Darwin or somewhere thereabouts, they claim they are refugees in need of assistance. It's ridiculous, of course. Barely ten years ago they were the enemy. Can you imagine what it would have been like if we had chartered large boats and sailed to England or Norway after the war and said we were German refugees in need of assistance? They would have arrested us on the spot. We knew what real refugees were like. Men and women with all their possessions and children in a wheelbarrow. Starving. Scrounging by the roadside for food or begging the occupation troops for scraps. They were refugees. If I were the prime minister of this country, I would build concentration camps in remote locations. Out in the desert perhaps. And whenever any of these boat people arrive, I whould lock them up inside the camps and allow them to send letters and photographs back to their families to deter others.'

'Indeed,' says Bormann, though personally he can't imagine such a thing every happening in Australia. The people here are hard for him to understand, refusing nationalistic fervour in favour of a philosophy of simple hedonism. He had always found it difficult to engage Australians in discussions of politics, but anybody would talk sports and real estate. They were quite unfathomable and he suspected that the first real question a government official would ask a refugee from Vietnam, in deciding to let him into the country or not, would be, what type of football they played.

'You do not agree?' asks Hitler.

'Perhaps yes. Perhaps no,' says Bormann, a past master of not making a commitment that might be held against him later. 'Different times require different tactics.'

And the Führer laughs. A single sharp bark that startles Blondi. 'History teaches us that all times are the same, but are just interpreted differently. If I was the leader of this country, I'd make a real nation out of it. I'd make people proud to stand up and salute the Australian flag. Have you seen the way they seem embarrassed by nationalism? They should have marches to celebrate their military victories over the Asiatic hordes of Vietnam. Instead they march to celebrate a defeat, at Gallipoli. Can you imagine the Germans marching to celebrate Stalingrad? Or El Alamein? Or Normandy?'

And Bormann has to admit he could not. Though he seems to recall that Vietnam was no less a defeat than Gallipoli.

'I'd instil a real sense of national pride into the people, using propaganda and a fear of the Asian hordes to the north. I'd instil a fear of Bolshevism and make it compulsory to fly the national flag. I'd insist that every new migrant to this country pass an exam that tested their values and loyalty!'

Bormann says nothing, thinking that if such an exam had been applied to them when they had entered the country, they might well have failed it and been sent back to Europe. 'Do you think there is enough groundswell support for a fascist state here?' Bormann asks, and he is thinking of the early years of the Nazi party, when they had to struggle to get followers and were only helped by national economic and political crises.

'Of course there is,' Hitler says. 'This country is full of petty fascists.'

'Is it?' asks Bormann, who has always found Australians strangely immune to most things political.

'I can walk you around any town and show you it is filled with petty fascists, waiting for an opportunity to be consolidated and organised into a movement. Parking inspectors. School administrators. Post office and bank clerks. Traffic police. Nightclub security guards. Train inspectors. Bus drivers. Primary school headmasters. Boy scout leaders. And sports administrators – we could people a fascist party in the nation just on sports administrators alone.'

Bormann fills his glass again and lets a minor stupor overcome him.

Then Hitler says, 'There is only one politician in this country who understands the principles of national socialism. He should be made prime minister.'

'Who is that?' Bormann asks.

'The premier of Queensland,' says Hitler. 'Joh Bjelke-Petersen. He understands the importance of maintaining a police state. He understands the importance of curtailing civil liberties and he understands the importance of surrounding himself with second-rate politicians who make him shine even more.'

Bormann is surprised to hear this and it shows on his face.

Again Hitler gives that single barking laugh. 'Did you think I was surrounded by men of talent?' he asks. And again he counts off on his fingers. 'Heinrich Himmler was a former chicken farmer. Göring was a drug-addled fop. Albert Speer had an artist's sensitive temperament. Goebbels was in love with his own rhetoric. And Bormann – he was a sycophantic bully who aligned himself with whichever way the wind changed.'

He sees Bormann's face and says quickly, 'I mean Albert Bormann, of course.' Then he says, 'Put on the television so we can see how the war is going.'

'*Jawohl*,' Bormann replies and struggles out of his seat.

He makes his way across to the old set, while Hitler tells him to be careful not to trip on the edge of the rug, where Blondi has been chewing it. Bormann examines the controls and twists the ON button.

A white square appears in the centre of the television and slowly expands to fill the screen. Bormann stands back to watch the picture come into clearer focus.

'Change the channel!' shouts Hitler. 'Quickly. Change the channel!'

Bormann looks down to see two German soldiers on the screen. One an officer and one an overweight soldier. The fat one says, 'I know nothing! Nothhhhhhing!' And the officer scowls.

'What is it?' asks Bormann.

'Idiot,' says Hitler. 'Have you never seen *Hogan's Heroes*? Change the channel. It is an insult to anyone who has ever served in the German army.'

Bormann says nothing. He has seen the program and it made him laugh.

'All the Germans are shown as idiots,' says Hitler, swinging one fist in the air. 'Perpetually being outwitted by the Americans. Always the Americans, as if nobody else fought in the war except them. And do you know where they learned this technique of propaganda using film? From Joseph Goebbels! He made films of all the Nazi glories and showed them around the nation. And then Leni Riefenstahl made her film of the Nuremberg rally. They were spectacular. And now look what the Americans are doing. An endless array of war movies where a small force of American soldiers is able to overcome a larger troop of Germans at every turn. Did you know, according to these propaganda pieces, that German soldiers can never shoot straight and can never hit an enemy target, even when using a machine gun, but an American soldier can hit a German soldier with a pistol at over a hundred yards, and kill him outright every time? And did you know that Germans are cruel to their prisoners, but the prisoners are canny and always manage to escape their prisons, while seemingly no Germans were ever taken prisoner and kept in camps in England or America? Did you know that? Well, if you sit up late at nights and watch the version of history you are served up on television, that is how you will invariably come to view things.'

His face is growing redder and redder. 'And the buffoons they choose to depict me are even worse. It is infuriating. It is demeaning. I know it is a fact that history is always written by the winners, but why must it be written in such a contemptuous manner as *Hogan's Heroes*?'

Bormann has changed the channel and is trying to see what program he has found. He looks back and is surprised to see the young boy is now sitting there in his seat.

And Hitler, who is obviously a keen fan of television, recognises it at once and says, 'Yes. Yes. *F-Troop*. This is much better.'

Uncle says that Mr Wright won't be coming at night, but I have asked him if I can stay just a little later this evening, just in case he does, because I don't want to miss things. Sometimes he comes round to visit Mummy at night. When the club has closed, he sometimes drives to our place and knocks on the door with this special knock that he has, so we always know it's him. Sometimes Mummy ignores him but sometimes she opens the door to talk to him. And sometimes she lets him come in. When she does, they go into her bedroom and lock the door and it sounds like they're fighting in there. I sit outside the door and want him to stop fighting with Mummy. I don't want him to hurt her. Then they stop and he goes home.

Sometimes he tries to be my friend and sometimes he doesn't. When he's trying to be friends, he gives me lollies or a packet of chips or something, and says that I should call him Uncle Michael, not Mister Wright. Then he tells Mummy that surely her mother told her she'd meet him one day. Mummy tells me that he thinks that is a joke. That he thinks he's pretty good. But she says he's a sleaze. She says that one day she'll tell his wife and kids about his visits.

I have noticed that she is more likely to let him into the house when she is feeling under the weather, and when I ask her why, she says gets lonely and needs a bit of company sometimes. I tell her that she has me for company and she says that is precious to her, but she needs the company of a man sometimes. I tell her that she should come and spend time with me and Uncle, as he's a man and I'm sure he would enjoy her company, but she just smiles and says that she hopes that one day I'll know what she means. I don't think I ever will, though. People are not like numbers. They change, so that when you think you know what they are like you find they might be different. They are full of perhapses. Even Uncle. I ask him if he'll let me fire one of the secret weapons and he says, 'Perhaps.' Even though he couldn't have built them without my help. Making secret weapons is like doing sums. You have to make sure that the hose lines for the petrol are the same size until they reach the end. And you have to make sure that any electric wires you use anywhere don't have any metal bits showing.

Uncle is good at coming up with ideas for secret weapons, but he's not so good at making them. Luckily he's got me to help him, though. We make a good team, he once told me. But that was before his old friend showed up. I hope he isn't going to stay too much longer. I might have to borrow one of Uncle's potato masher bungers, blow up Mr Wright's letter box and tell the police it was Uncle's friend who did it. He wouldn't be too young to go to jail. Then things could be just like they were before.

Then Uncle calls me over to him. He has me stand before him and he tells me what a good and brave boy I am, and he reaches out and puts one hand on my cheek. Then he says I should return to the front lines. I ask him what that means and he says I remind him of a boy he knew many years ago. A boy who was also brave and good and who faced down the approaching enemy. Then he says it means I should go home and look after my mummy now.

When I go home, Mother is under the weather again, but at least Mr Wright doesn't come around, knocking on the door with his special knock like it's a secret code or something.

Zwölf

The art of leadership…consists in consolidating the attention of the
people…and taking care that nothing will split up that attention.

– Mein Kampf

The television news of the Falklands is not good, thinks Bormann, but
Hitler is ecstatic.

'The endgame is upon them,' he says. 'The pincers of the trap are
poised to close on the British forces.'

As Bormann sees it, the British are on the verge of capturing Port
Stanley and over-running the Argentinian troops.

'This is going to be a momentous time ahead of us,' Hitler says.
'We will rise up, taking them all by surprise and once more assume our
destinies. He stabs his finger in the air. 'Yes. Our destinies!' Then Hitler
reaches down to the coffee table and pushes aside an old newspaper
and pulls out a well-thumbed paperback. 'Have you read this book?'
he asks.

Bormann looks at the cover, *SS-GB*, and he has to admit that he
has not.

'It is a story about how we should have invaded and occupied Great
Britain,' Hitler says. 'The populace are under our heel and have to
conform to German ways of doing things. There is all this nonsense
about the SS and the army being intense rivals, and battling each
other to get the British nuclear scientists under their control, but it is
otherwise just how it should have been.'

He passes the book to Bormann, who flicks through it. There are
many passages underlined, and German translations of words written
in the margin in pencil. He stops and reads one passage that has been

heavily underlined: 'Members of Parliament and members of the puppet government who had learned to play their role in the new Nazi super-state that covered most of Europe.'

'The Nazi super-state,' he says and Hitler nods. Bormann quite likes the sound of that. It was something that really could have happened too. If Hitler hadn't kept trusting bumbling idiots like Göring and Himmler and instead had given more military power to Bormann.

'It is how it could still be,' Hitler says. 'Imagine it, German and Argentinian troops stationed outside the British parliament and Big Ben, with the Argentinian and Nazi flags flying side by side.'

And Bormann begins to wonder if perhaps the Führer might be right. Surely there is still a chance. By surprise attacks, his leader has shown previously that it is possible to pluck a victory from the jaws of defeat. He has often told Bormann that war is a battle of wills, and the dominant will always triumphs over the lesser. *Triumph of the Will* is what Leni Riefenstahl had called her film of the Nazi Nuremburg rallies of 1934.

Bormann looks across at Hitler and is about to tell him something about those wonderful films of so many soldiers marching under torchlight when Hitler finally asks Bormann that question he has been dreading.

'So tell me about Doctor Mengele,' he says. 'Is he living in the presidential palace? Does he wear an Argentinian military uniform? Is he still obsessing about twins?'

Everything goes out of Bormann's mind as his fanciful imaginings snap shut, like a clam closing tight, or the jaws of a trap. He says, guardedly, 'The last time I met with him we talked of other things than twins.'

'The future. Not the past. Correct? He was always a visionary. I keep all his letters here, you know.'

'Is that wise?' asks Bormann.

'We write in code.'

'Of course.' He licks his lips, wishing he were a little less cloudy-headed for this conversation, and asks, 'And, ah, when was the last correspondence you received from him?'

'Quite recently,' says Hitler. 'I will fetch it.' And he shuffles over to a jumble-strewn desk and searches amongst the papers there for some moments. Then he brings back a letter and holds it out Bormann. 'See how cleverly he disguises his identity,' the Führer says.

Bormann holds the letter at arm's length and adjusts his glasses. It is a letter advertising a lottery draw for four houses in Queensland. There are pictures of the houses and the slogan, 'Your Future is Here'. He reads over the details offering tickets in the draw and says, 'And this is from him. You are certain?'

'Of course,' says the Führer. 'It is a code telling me that the dawning of the Fourth Reich is upon us.'

Bormann nods solemnly.

'I have others,' says Hitler, waving in the direction of the desk. 'Taken one by one, you might not see anything in them, but when you link them together, you see his clever plan.' He shuffles over and brings back another letter offering a herbal remedy guaranteed to keep one young. 'Mengele has finally solved the genetic puzzle of mankind. How to prolong life! See. It is clearly stated here.' He stabs a finger at the letter.

Bormann nods again.

'Mengele has been my emissary with the Argentinian military. After their undoubted victory in the Falklands, or Malvinas as we should now call them, he will call for me to join him there. We will once more march on Paris, don't you see?'

Bormann does not see, but he says, 'Of course. It is a brilliant plan.'

Hitler allows himself a moment of gloating. Then he asks, 'Do you know how to say *Sieg Heil* in Spanish?'

And Bormann has to admit that he does not.

'That is a pity,' says Hitler. 'I find many of the phrases I would need to learn are not on the language records.' Again he rises awkwardly to his feet and shuffles across to the TV, turning down the volume and then moving across to the record player. He fumbles with the dials for a moment and then returns to sit beside Bormann.

The voice of a highly educated English man says, 'Please repeat the phrase after it is spoken.'

Then a Spanish voice says, '*Buenos Dias!*'

'*Buenos Dias*,' says Hitler and then as an aside to Bormann, 'Good day.'

'*Como esta usted?*' says the voice.

'*Como esta usted?*' Hitler says. 'How are you?'

'*Muy bien, gracias*,' say the voice.

'*Muy bien, gracias*,' says Hitler. 'Very well, thank you.'

'*Donde es el bano?*' the record says.

'*Donde es el bano?*' Hitler says. 'Where is the train station?'

'Uh – I believe it actually means where is the toilet?' says Bormann.

Hitler scowls at him. 'Absurd,' he says.

And then he shushes Bormann while he continues with his basic Spanish lesson, while on the television Bormann watches a news update showing a line of Argentinian soldiers surrendering to the British with their hands on their heads.

'*Hay una corrida hoy*,' says Hitler, repeating after the recorded voice. 'Is there a bullfight today?'

Eventually the record ends and Hitler turns to Bormann, and says, 'Tell me about life in South America. Tell me what it will be like.'

And Bormann looks at his Führer and says, 'It will be like everything you imagine and more. The Argentinians have a love of military splendour. You will be able to stand on the balcony of the Casa Rosada and look out over the military parades on the Plaza del Mayo there. Rows and rows of helmeted soldiers all saluting you with a cheer that you can feel inside your chest.'

Hitler nods enthusiastically.

'Buenos Aires is a very European city,' Bormann says. 'You would swear parts of it had been designed by Albert Speer. There is the grand boulevard the Avenue of 9 July. It is obviously based on your own great autobahns and has eight lanes running for several miles. It is spectacular to drive down. And of course the Argentinians have a great love of the German people. You would remember how much the president Juan Peron expressed his support for National Socialism and based his own rise to power on your own strategies.'

Hitler nods quite fervently. Entranced by the vision.

'Military governments dominate most of South America, with occasional failed experiments in democracy,' Bormann says. 'The political strength in Brazil and Argentina and Chile and Paraguay is all in the military. Old Nazis gather in cafés and bars, openly mixing, telling stories of the past and of the future. And they are adulated by the young of South America. They treat these men as oracles. They know they can show them the path to the future.'

'Go on,' says Hitler.

But Bormann is running out of the will to go on. All he can say, once more, is, 'It will be everything you imagine.'

It is quite dark outside when Bormann eventually steers the conversation around to something he has been trying to raise since his arrival. 'Have you had any contact with your ratline handlers in the last years?' he asks.

And Hitler shakes his head. 'My ratline handlers are all dead or retired,' he says. 'Whenever I have tried to contact the security agencies, they pass me onto a young upstart or office lackey who knows nothing about my code names and how valuable I have been to them. I'm tempted sometimes to simply ask, "Do you know who you are talking to?" But I know the power of my name. It is like a mystical word that evokes fear and loathing. Indeed it is no longer a name. It is an incantation.' He frowns deeply and sighs. 'That a simple family name could have such power. World leaders would sell their souls for that. Thatcherism. Reaganomics. Can you imagine those ever invoking fear and loathing? Do they have the power to unsettle millions? I doubt it.'

Bormann suspects that to some they might, but he says nothing. He knows what the Führer means, though. The name Hitler is more than a name. It is a burden of greatness to be borne by this man alone, despite the petty envy of those who have surrounded him. But it is incumbent upon him to tell the Führer what he has come here to tell him.

'When we rise again to power, those young security analysts will shake their heads and wonder where we could have been hiding all these years. They will be lining up to curry favour with us then. A new world is rising, Bormann, and it will lift us like a Zeppelin, bearing us aloft once more.'

Bormann wants to agree with Hitler, wants to see the vision too, but he has a sudden moment of clarity, like that which carried him across the oceans to this quiet town by the end of the world, and he steels himself and says, softly, '*Mein Führer*, there are certain things I must inform you of. I have been travelling widely, as you know, and talking to those who have supported us in exile, and I must report that many things have changed in the last few years. There is a strong feeling that, despite what international politics might suggest, the cold war is starting to unravel. Many analysts predict it ending by the end of this decade. And I'm sure you know what that means.' He pauses a moment, but now that he has started speaking the words are tumbling out. 'The Western intelligence agencies will no longer have need of us. They assisted our escape from Europe for their own self-interests to assist them in their war against communism. But if the war against communism is gone, what need have they to protect us any more? And, as you say, our ratline handlers in the church and in Western governments are largely dead or retired. Those who have replaced them have no need to protect us. In fact, it is in their interests now to uncover us and prosecute us.

'*Mein Führer*,' he says. 'These are dangerous times for us. Even in South America it is becoming more and more difficult to find regimes willing to protect us. General Stroessner in Paraguay will remain an ally, but in truth, his country is verging on becoming a backwater. There is no future for us there. Do you see what I am saying?' he asks. 'Can you see that the future is upon us already and it is going to be a very different world that will have no place for us, except to strip away our cover, dig us out of hiding and prosecute us in public trials even more degrading than Eichmann's. They will put us on the world stage and make circus exhibits of us. There is no future in Argentina. They will lose the war in the Falklands and the military government there will fall because of it. Do you see this?'

Bormann looks across at his Führer, and he sees that he does not see, for he is asleep, his dentures sliding out of his mouth. Bormann looks glumly at Hitler and then rises to his feet. He needs to pee and his knees are not up to a walk both up and down the stairs to the guest bathroom. He looks at his sleeping leader, and licks his lips quickly, that fast flicking motion, and he tiptoes down the hallway to the Führer's toilet. It will be an honour to use it, he thinks. Inside, he sees it has a very nice wooden seat and the walls are pasted with cuttings from newspapers. Bormann has to squint, without his glasses, to see that they are a mix of horoscopes and New Age prophecies of how a strong leader will rise to take over the world.

And suddenly Bormann is struck by how pitiful the old Nazis he keeps in contact with actually are. And he is as pitiful as any of them. They have become paranoid old men, often living in poverty and isolation, filled with an unending fear of being kidnapped by Israeli agents. And that makes him think once more of his last meeting with Doctor Mengele. It was no different. He sighs deeply and shakes his shrivelled old penis, to try and coax a little more piss from his aged swollen prostate-blocked bladder.

There are still some days when he feels that a single individual can make a difference to the future of the world, but there are others, like tonight, when he thinks it all hopeless and they are living in a past that will never be returned to them. But a man needs to do whatever he can, he decides, even if all that he can do at that particular moment is flush the toilet. Then he covers his Führer with a blanket and goes downstairs to bed.

Bormann wakes in the darkness and sees the dim outline of somebody sitting on the bed. '*Mein Führer?*' he asks.

But the figure is too tall. He turns to Bormann and says, 'Shhh! No moving!' It is Joseph Mengele.

'Impossible,' mutters Bormann.

'Nothing is impossible to men of great destiny,' says Mengele. 'Didn't the Führer teach you anything?'

'But how?' asks Bormann.

'I said no moving,' Mengele repeats.

And then Bormann looks down to see what he is doing. He is surprised to see that his chest cavity is wide open. Mengele is operating on him.

'What are you doing?' Bormann asks meekly.

'Improving you,' says Mengele. 'Taking out the old worn-out bits and putting in new ones. You'll be like a ten-year-old boy when I've finished with you.'

Bormann nods. 'Of course.' He would like to be a young boy again. Would like the simplicity of things.

'Look at this,' says Mengele, lifting out something that looks like a compass.'

'What is it?' asks Bormann.

'Your moral compass,' says Mengele. 'But it's been broken for years.' He tosses it over his shoulder. 'That will free up a bit of space. And there's this too.' He pulls out something small and hard, shaped like a walnut.

'What is that?' asks Bormann.

'Your courage,' says Mengele. 'You'll need a lot more than that.' He reaches under the bed and pulls out an iron cross. He pushes it into Bormann's chest and pins it to his lung or something. 'Hm,' says Mengele. 'Not quite enough yet.'

He pulls out another iron cross and pins that to Bormann's stomach. 'How's that?' he asks him. 'Do you feel brave enough yet?'

'Brave enough for what?' asks Bormann, although of course he knows.

'Obviously not,' says Mengele and pins a third iron cross to his insides.

Bormann closes his eyes. Mengele could fill his insides with medals but he still won't feel brave enough for what he has to do.

Dreizehn

There must be no majority decision, but only responsible persons, and the word 'council' must be restored to its original meaning. Surely every man will have advisers by his side, the decision will be made by one man.

– Mein Kampf

Martin Bormann wakes in the dark with a shout, his hands clutching at his chest. He was having a bad dream, he thinks. A dream of visiting the Führer in a small remote fishing town in Australia, and finding him living a delusion. And he was contributing to it. He tries to go back to sleep but finds it hard to breathe. He knows it is that weight of his conscience pressing on him. It is an unfamiliar feeling, of course, and takes him some while to understand it. But he has deceived his Führer. It is a betrayal of his position. A betrayal of his leader's trust in him. And men have been hung by their balls for less. He resolves that he will tell the Führer the truth about Doctor Mengele in the morning, and sometime in the early hours he finally drifts off to sleep and dreams of the Gestapo finding him using Hitler's toilet and dragging him to a cell for interrogation, where they play *Hogan's Heroes* repeats endlessly and accuse him of being responsible for them.

Bormann wakes at ten a.m. sharp to the sound of Hitler's toilet flushing and the pipes by his head rattling. It takes him some time to struggle out of bed however, as he is feeling more than his age today. He sits there on the edge of the bed and takes an inventory of his aches. His knees are still sore. His head is woolly. His tongue is bloated and dry in his mouth. He has an ache in the small of his back. He hasn't passed a good stool in two days, and his bladder is bursting. It is going to be a long day. He sighs and climbs to his feet.

He will start the day with a shower, he thinks, and he goes to the small cubicle without a curtain by the toilet. He takes off his clothes and looks at his aged and weary body. Talk about betrayals, he thinks. His body finds a new way to turn against him each day. And then, for the first time in many, many years, he thinks of those photographs he has seen of the lines of naked people lining up to enter the shower blocks. Those grainy black and white pictures that show men and women holding their hands over their genitals, as if protecting their modesty at that moment would make a difference. He sighs again and turns on the shower. The pipes rattle and a hiss of air comes out of the shower nozzle. Bormann feels his insides turn cold. It couldn't possibly be, he thinks. 'No,' he shouts, just as the water finally fills the empty pipes and a burst of cold water splashes across his face like a slap.

Bormann finally drags himself up the stairs about fifteen minutes later, to find Hitler bent over the dining table, busily working on something. '*Mein Führer,*' he says, determined to say what he has to before he is distracted by another of Hitler's rambling discourses.

'Come in, come in,' Hitler says. 'Things are moving at a great pace.'

'There are things I need to tell you,' Bormann says.

'Later, later,' says Hitler, waving at him with a dismissive hand. 'Come and see the pace of the battle.'

'*Mein Führer,*' Bormann almost pleads.

But Hitler is no longer listening to him and talks over him. 'Look here,' he says, pointing at his diagrams and maps. 'The British have moved closer upon the settlement of Port Stanley in the night. There was a fierce battle at this place, Mount Tumbledown.' And he stabs at his map with his index finger. 'An appropriate name for a defeat of the over-confident, is it not? It overlooks Port Stanley, see, and is the last effective point of the outer defences. And it is here that the British troops have come undone. The TV news says there is a blackout on reporting details of the battle, which as we both know means it is bad news. This is it! The Argentinians are beginning their counter-thrust against an overconfident and over-extended enemy. You will recall we did exactly the same thing against the Allies in the Ardennes offensive in late 1944.'

Bormann is certain that that offensive, the last major push against the Western allies in the war, the Battle of the Bulge as it was known, was a failure. But he is still feeling a little off-colour and has enough doubt about the strength of his memory not to mention it.

'You draw the enemy in and then crush him,' Hitler says, and pounds the table. 'It is what I ordered my generals to do against the Russians. But the cowards betrayed me! I should have had them all shot on the spot!'

Hitler looks up at Bormann and says, working himself up into a rage again, 'It was all the generals' fault, of course. They were forever advising caution in all things. Saying we were not ready to advance. Saying that we were putting our flanks in danger. Saying that my plans were over-ambitious. And yet, whenever I disregarded their advice, we had great victories. They were like old women, bickering all the time.' He sighs and his head drops forward in a position of deep dismay. 'I should have followed Stalin's lead and had all the senior generals shot!' he mumbles.

And Bormann does recall how the generals in the bunker would almost beat their heads on the walls in frustration with the Führer, who was forever changing his mind. Deciding to advance. Then deciding not to. Moving troops to the east. Then moving them back to the west. Sometimes immobilised by indecision. Or, he wonders again, is that just how he remembers it?

'*Mein Führer*,' he tries yet again, but Hitler is now engrossed in his maps once more. 'The Argentinians will have divisions hidden in the hills here to the north,' he says. 'Or perhaps they are in Port Stanley itself, out of sight from aerial reconnaissance. That will be the secret to their success,' he says. 'Surprise.'

Then he says to Bormann, 'Do you remember when we invaded France, how the French and British were massed against the Belgium border and instead we attacked through the forest paths of the French

Ardennes?' They were too shocked to know how to respond. That has been a prime principle of my life. Never let the enemy take you by surprise.'

'*Mein Führer*,' says Bormann again. More urgently now.

'Not now,' says Hitler.

'Yes, now,' says Bormann, with a tone of voice he has never dared use to his Führer before.

Hitler looks up at him in surprise and, looking out of the window, Bormann says, in a much softer voice, 'The council are here!'

Hitler stands up and sees the two council vehicles pull into his driveway. Councillor Wright climbs out of one car holding a sheet of paper in his hands.

'Quickly! To our defensive positions!' Hitler says.

As the councillor and his men make their way across the front lawn towards the stairs to the upper front door, Hitler leads Bormann and Blondi down the inside stairs to the lower part of the house. Hitler throws open the door of a box on the wall that looks like a fuse box. Inside are levers and buttons, with labels in German.

'Our first line of surprise attack is the wall of flame,' says Hitler, and his shaking hands dance across the controls. He presses one button and pulls a lever.

Bormann hears the distinctive wump sound of petrol igniting. There is a cry of alarm, but it is not the cry of men running around on fire.

The Führer looks concerned. He flips open a small flap on the wall to reveal an observation slit, masked by a tiny air vent, looking out onto the front yard. '*Donner und Blitzen*!' he exclaims. 'I ignited the petrol too early!'

Bormann tries to peer out the observation slit too. He can see the lawn sprinkler, turning, gushing out flames about a metre long, like some circus trick. The council men are jumping around and crying out, but still advancing upon the house.

'No matter,' says Hitler. 'We shall take advantage of the distraction this causes to launch our second offensive line of defence.'

He presses another button on the panel and Bormann hears an explosion. But it is not the sound of a bomb. It is more the sound of a large firecracker going off.

'*Teuffel.*' spits Hitler, and slams the observation hatch before Bormann can get a glimpse of what has happened. 'I never should have bought those explosives in the post from China! No wonder they lost the Korean war.'

'What shall we do?' Bormann asks.

'We shall make a strategic advance backwards to the bunker and wait for the car bomb to explode as they try and force their way into the shed. Just one moment and I will prime it.' He presses another button and then closes the door on the box. 'Come,' he says to both Bormann and Blondi, and leads them to a tiny cupboard by the wall. He fumbles with a key, opens the cupboard door and steps in.

Bormann follows. The cupboard conceals a cleverly camouflaged door that opens onto the backyard. Keeping low, the two old men scuttle across the overgrown lawn towards the shed.

Bormann has a quick glimpse of the front yard as they near the shed. He sees the small fire display from the sprinkler and sees there is a bit of statue rubble on the driveway. The council workers must all be in the house by now. Hitler fiddles with the lock and then they are inside the safety of the shed.

Once safely down in the bunker, Hitler bolts the door behind them, switches on the light and Bormann finds he is quite giddy from the excitement of it all. Hitler has had him carry the bulky death ray down the stairs and he is puffing, so he tells him to sit in an old couch to get his breath back. It is a kindly gesture, thinks Bormann. The Führer of old would never have offered him a seat. He would have expected him to be there at his beck and call twenty-four hours a day. And he was. He was Hitler's shadow in those days, perpetually trying to second-guess his every need and translating his obscure rants into orders for the day. They needed each other, he thinks, like the killer whales and the whalers.

Hitler then slumps into a chair of his own and says, 'Now we wait.'

Bormann closes his eyes and breathes in the musty concrete-dust air and Hitler says exactly what is on his own mind. 'Do you ever think back on those last days in the Berlin bunker?'

'Constantly,' says Bormann, without opening his eyes. And in this he knows that he undoubtedly re-enacts the past to try and make it turn out better just as much as the Führer does.

'Do you know,' says Hitler, 'I expected the tide of war to turn suddenly in our favour when President Roosevelt died. What date was that?'

'It was 12 April,' says Bormann. 'Two weeks before the end.'

'Ah yes,' says Hitler. 'I believed we were witnessing a miracle like the one that saved the reign of Frederick the Great from the crushing forces of Tsarina Elizabeth of Russia during the Seven Years' war. Did you know that Frederick was on the verge of killing himself with poison when he heard that the Tsarina had unexpectedly died, leading to the withdrawal of the Russian troops?'

'We heard the news of Roosevelt's death the same day we first heard the Russian guns around Berlin,' Bormann says.

'It was our ill fortune that it was not Stalin who died,' Hitler says. 'That would have changed everything.'

Bormann remembers how the massed forces of the Russians steadily drove the brave German defenders back each day as they incessantly encircled Berlin. By the Führer's birthday on 20 April, there were less than 100,000 soldiers defending the city, and too many of those were old men or children. And all the while there was a glut of officers and officials crammed into the many bunkers and tunnels beneath the Reich Chancellery.

'Do you remember my fifty-fifth birthday celebration?' Hitler asks.

'Of course,' says Bormann. 'Göring, Himmler and Speer were there to celebrate with you. I remember the main topic of conversation was that everyone was urging you to leave Berlin while it was still not too late.'

'Yes. That's right,' says Hitler. 'Some wanted me to go north, some wanted me to go south. But I decided to stay on and fight.'

Bormann seems to recall that it was Hitler himself who was struck by indecision, but says nothing. 'You held the last official briefing two days later,' he says. 'I remember that well. You abused the army for letting the Reich down.' In his memory, Hitler had ranted and expelled everybody from the briefing room when told that the counter-attack against the Russians had not occurred as there were not enough troops available, and he had accused the generals of treason, then had collapsed to the floor.

'Those cowards,' says Hitler. 'Defeatists all of them.'

Bormann also remembers how he forbade any of the military from seeing the Führer from that point, as he felt it was he himself who was now keeping his leader going. He had assumed the responsibility for the future of the Fatherland.

'Even without the generals you continued to fight,' Bormann says.

'I recall that you and Goebbels mobilised civilians across the city to drive back the Russians,' Hitler says.

'We did,' Bormann says, without adding that the poorly armed and untrained recruits were slaughtered almost to a man by the advancing Russians, despite the military courts that authorised the hanging of anybody in the streets seen to be acting in a defeatist manner, hanging signs around their necks saying things like 'I have been hanged because I did not believe in the Führer.'

'And Blondi had pups,' says Hitler. 'Do you remember that?'

'Yes,' says Bormann. 'Of course. There were the four pups. And the six Goebbels children moved into the bunker about the same time.'

'That improved everybody's morale,' says Hitler. 'The spirit of the young is undefeatable.' He looks about, as if expecting to see the boy Adam playing quietly in a corner. But it is just the two old men and their memories.

Bormann recalls how on 23 April, only a few days before the end, when the last road out of Berlin to the north-west was in danger of being closed, even the Hitler Youth were mobilised in defence of the city. Armed largely with just anti-tank rockets they stood vainly against the Russian hordes and they too were cut to pieces. But he can recall one young boy being brought into the bunker who had destroyed a Russian tank, and they made such a fuss over him, all those generals and officers, patting his head and pinching his cheek. He looked shell-shocked and dazed. They pinned a medal on him and sent him back out to fight.

'Yes,' says Bormann, 'The spirit of the young is undefeatable.'

'Do you know, I find I can still recall the last days in great detail,' says Hitler, 'though many things that happened to me this week are not as clear.'

And Bormann thinks it odd the things you forget, and the things you can't forget. 'On 25 April, the first Russian artillery shells hit the bunker,' says Bormann, 'and we had to shut down the air-conditioning for a time because of all the cement dust being sent throughout the bunker.'

'On 26 April, General Ritten von Greim and Hanna Reitsch flew in over the Russian lines for his official appointment as head of the Luftwaffe,' says Hitler. 'They were a brave pair. Do you remember they were hit and von Greim was wounded and Hanna Reitsch landed the plane by leaning over his body to take the controls from him?'

'They were the bravest of the brave,' says Bormann. It was a surprise enough that they had managed to fly into Berlin, but they also managed to fly out again. 'They were the last to leave Berlin, were they not?' says Bormann.

'Well, apart from us,' says Hitler.

Bormann shakes his head, as if the flight from Berlin were all a dream.

Hitler sees his face change and says, 'You were my stalwart, though. Finding traitors all about me. Even at the last moments. You showed me how treacherous Göring had been, and even drafted the order to have him expelled from the party. You were also the one who showed me that Himmler was attempting to negotiate a peace treaty with the Allies.'

And Bormann can remember searching for traitors everywhere. Accusing everyone of letting Hitler down as the Russians got closer and closer. As if, somehow, by blaming the right person, everything could be reversed again. Bormann was right to see traitors all about them. If they had remained resolute, surely things would have ended differently. Surely.

'The generals were not pushing the enemy hard enough,' Bormann says. 'They refused to believe in you. They were defeatists!'

All the talk in the Bunker amongst the soldiers was of organising a break-out. Of deserting the Führer and trying to break through the Russian lines and reach the Allies so they could surrender to them.

'On 28 April the Russians were only one kilometre away and we had to ban anybody from going up into the garden,' Bormann says. 'Telling them there was too big a risk of being hit by shell fire. But in reality it was to stop them from running away.'

But Hitler has another memory. 'That was the day of my wedding,' he says.

And Bormann puts his hands over his eyes. To black out that memory or perhaps to cement it from fading. He doesn't know any more. Poor Eva. The wedding was such a rushed ceremony, performed late on the night of 28 April, so near the end now. He and Goebbels were the witnesses. Most people in the bunker complex were unaware of it. It occurred in Hitler's private bunker chambers on the lower level, which were largely kept separate to the rest of the bunker. Such a short ceremony and the pair were wed. Although, Bormann recalls, the Führer still kept referring to her as Fräulein Braun afterwards. He suspects, though he never asked, that the marriage was the one thing that Eva had begged of Hitler, and the favour he finally granted her. It was the only place he did not have full access to the Führer – in his bedchamber.

There had been a lot of speculation about Hitler and Eva Braun's intimate life, of course, but Bormann had no evidence as to whether their relationship was consummated or not. Hitler was genuinely affectionate towards Eva, but not in the same way he cared about Geli, he was certain. And he wonders if the Führer misses her sometimes and regrets how things had turned out. He should ask him, he thinks. For if not now, when?

But Hitler says first, 'There is something I'd like to ask you.'

'Of course, *mein Führer*,' says Bormann, opening his eyes and looking at him. 'Anything.'

'You keep in touch with things. You know where all the old hands are hiding out. You know where all the skeletons are buried, correct?'

'Well, some of the skeletons perhaps.' He is not sure what the Führer is getting at and is, as is his nature, cautious about over-committing himself to an answer.

'You must hear things about the whereabouts of people.'

'I try and keep informed.'

'There is somebody I'd like to know about.'

'Of course. One of the party?'

'No. Not one of the party.'

Bormann waits for him to say the name, but when he does say it, he cannot keep the surprise from his face.

'My sister Paula,' says Hitler. 'Do you know how she is?'

Bormann looks down at his feet and fiddles with his fingers. '*Mein Führer*,' he says, 'yes, I do know. But it is not good news. It is quite sad, in fact. You must console yourself to her fate.'

Hitler sets his mouth in a grim line and waits for Bormann to say it.

'She died in 1960,' he says. 'She lived out her last years under the name of Paula Wolff.'

Hitler gives the smallest of nods.

'But even at the end she was unwaveringly faithful to you,' says Bormann. 'She said in time you would be recognised to be as great a military genius as Napoleon.'

'She never married?' he asks.

'No.'

'Did you know,' Hitler says, 'that I had her wartime fiancé sent to the Eastern front and he never returned?'

'I did not know that,' Bormann says.

'He worked in a hospital and was in charge of killing the disabled who were brought in to him.'

'I did not know that either,' Bormann says.

'So you think he'd be a reasonable chap. But I never liked him much.' Hitler is pensive for some time and then says, 'It is ironic, because my brother Alois's son, Heinz Hitler, was a great Nazi, and he volunteered to fight for the cause and was taken prisoner on the eastern front and died there. He was a good Aryan. He would have carried on the family name.'

'I was sorry when I heard that he had died,' Bormann says. 'He was a good boy.'

'So I am the last Hitler left alive,' he says sadly.

'No,' says Bormann a little too quickly. 'There is still William Patrick Hitler.'

The look that comes upon the Führer's face tells him at once that he has said something the Führer did not wish to hear.

'That…that…rogue!' snaps Hitler. 'He is a disgrace to the family name.'

'Well, he was never fully German, was he?' says Bormann, trying to toady his way out of trouble.

'I signed an order some time ago, I am certain, forbidding anybody to ever mention his name in my presence.'

'It must have slipped my mind,' says Bormann.

And he remembers the one and only time he had met William Patrick Hitler, or Willie, as he liked to be called. He was the son of Alois Hitler's first wife. An Irishwoman named Brigitte. He had come to Germany before the war to cash in on his surname. He asked Hitler for money and favours and wanted to go to parties and meet girls and get drunk. He was a wastrel. A crude-mouthed playboy. But Hitler had given him money. There was some talk of blackmail involved. And then, during the war, he had the audacity to go to America and cash in on the family name with the enemy!

'Did he have any children?' the Führer suddenly asks.

'Four boys, I believe.'

'Then there is some hope that the Hitler name will still continue into the next centuries?'

In fact, Bormann knows, they were all ashamed to bear the name, and each one of them had changed it.

'But you will outlive them all,' Bormann says.

'So Mengele assures me,' says Hitler.

'Ah, yes,' says Bormann and looks at the ground again. Tries not to fiddle overly with this hands.

'Have you kept in contact with your own children?' the Führer asks him. 'I recall you had many children. Eight, was it?'

'Ten,' says Bormann.

Hitler nods a little in admiration. 'Did they survive the war?'

And now Bormann has to fight to keep the emotion out of his voice as he says, 'All but two. One girl died shortly after birth and another died in 1946. They were raised anonymously in foster homes and are spread all over the place now. I don't visit them but I try to keep up to date on their activities.' Bormann runs over their names in his head, something he has not done for many years. Adolf, Isle, Rudolf, Heinrich. Eva. Gerda, Fred and Volker. Mostly named after Nazi officials. Then he realises he has missed one, but can't remember which.

'I hope they have done well for themselves,' says Hitler. 'I recall one was named after both you and me. Adolf Martin Bormann.'

'Yes. He was your godson,' says Bormann.

'Of course,' says Hitler. 'What happened to him? Did he turn out as ambitious as his father?'

Bormann takes a deep breath. It was one of his many secrets that his last communication with his wife Gerda was a telegram ordering her to kill their children and then herself. 'He became a priest for a time, perhaps because he knew how much I disliked the clergy.' And he has always wondered if she had told the children as they grew up. 'But later he left it and married a nun.'

'He bedded a nun?' says Hitler. 'Surely just as ambitious as his father then.'

'Well, a former nun.'

'Ah.'

'Yes,' says Bormann. Then he says, 'Germany would have rejoiced if our Führer had had children.'

'Eva would have liked to,' Hitler says softly. It is the first time he has spoken her name. 'But it was quite impossible!' he says.

And Bormann wonders for a moment if that was due to the pressures of office or the fact that Hitler really did only have one left testicle. But then he catches himself and remembers that was a malicious rumour. Like Goebbels having no balls at all. Obviously not the case since he had six children.

Ah, those poor children, he thinks. The shock of knowing that their own mother had poisoned them ran around the bunker like a shell blast. Even Bormann was shocked by the reality of it. The thought of the gesture he found brave, but knowing the dead children were in a room so close to them was horrific. Perhaps his own wife Gerda had been braver in defying him. And he can picture the faces of the Goebbels children better than he can recall his own children. Helga, Hilde, Helmut, Holdine, Hedda and Heidrun.

It was said that Magda Goebbels was madly in love with Hitler, and chose all her children's names starting with an H in his honour. It was also said that Eva Braun knew this and guarded him more jealously than Blondi had. There were so many things said, of course, and after so many years he sometimes found it hard to quite remember which were the facts and which were not. He is sure he can remember Magda Goebbels proclaiming that a life without National Socialism was a life not worth living. That would have been on her last day – 1 May. After Eva was already dead. The Russians were only a few hundred metres away now and the few German troops were being crushed under the overwhelming might of the Russian tanks.

Hitler first had his doctor poison Blondi, though he chose not to witness it. And Bormann can remember that it appeared to upset him more than the death of Eva had. That was the previous day – 30 April. He had one of the secretaries type up his will and then he and Eva went into his chambers. They were all very worn and tired, having been woken by Russian artillery about five a.m. Hitler had instructed Bormann to give strict orders to the Führer's personal adjutant, Otto Günsche, on what to do with the bodies. He was to wrap them in blankets, carry them up to the garden and there burn their remains. They could barely find enough petrol to do the job.

That was the first time that Hitler had actually seen his double. Bormann had had the Gestapo search all over the country to find men that bore a close enough resemblance to the Führer that they could be coached to take his place in brief public appearances. After that failed bomb plot at his Wolf's Lair headquarters in Rastenburg in July 1944, Hitler was afraid to go out in public. Let the doubles take the bombs and the bullets, he had said.

That was where the idea had come to him. But the Führer wouldn't agree at first. He was convinced he should kill himself rather than risk being captured and publicly humiliated. Bormann thought he was going to go through with it too. Right up until the last moment. Something changed his mind at the very edge of the precipice. Some desire to live.

'Did Eva know?' Bormann suddenly asks Hitler.

But the Führer is unable to answer him. Bormann looks at him closely in the dim light of the bunker and wonders if it is tears that he can see in his eyes.

'Ah, Eva,' Hitler says. 'She was quite a dunce, but her simple optimism was something that kept everyone's hope alive in those last days. I told her it would be painless. Told her we would die together. She swallowed the poison willingly and didn't even live to see my double brought in.'

Bormann had him kept in a small room, drugged, for days. They left him there on the couch by Eva. Then Bormann left the room so that there would be absolutely no witnesses. 'I crunched the poison capsule between his teeth and then pressed my gun to his head and fired,' Hitler says. 'It was three-thirty p.m.' He pauses and Bormann can hear the sounds of his laboured breathing. 'You might think that the only time I've shot a man,' Hitler says. 'But I was a soldier in the First World War, remember. I had a life before we met that you can only guess at. And my life since we parted is something else you'll probably never know.'

Bormann has never heard him talk like this.

Hitler takes a deep breath and says, 'There are so many nights I wished that Eva had escaped with me. Just to have someone to talk to about those days. Just to have someone.' He takes another long deep breath and then says, 'But it is the Führer's destiny to be alone. He is not to be distracted by mortal needs. He must live above other humans.' Then he says to Bormann, 'Do you remember the night of the break-out?'

'Of course,' says Bormann. It was the closest he had ever been to combat. 'We left the bunker shortly before midnight, in two groups. The women were dressed as soldiers, as were you. Nobody could tell who was who in the dark. We made our way through the underground tunnels to Friedrichstrasse station, where we split up into smaller groups. Some made it through. Some were shot down on the Weidendamm Bridge. I went on with you and Artur Axmann, who could do nothing to stop the bands of his crazed Hitler Youth shooting at anything that moved in the darkness.'

'It was so dark and confusing,' says Hitler. 'I could not recognise Berlin. Everything was in ruins.'

'We found a boat and took to the river.'

'But we heard Russian voices ahead of us and pulled into the shore.'

'We could hear the shrieks and cries of German girls being raped and molested by the Russians.'

'We decided to travel along the railway line.'

'And we could hear those bands of maddened Hitler Youth shooting at anybody older than them.'

'Axmann said he would scout ahead.'

'He came back and said there were Russians that way too.'

'We decided to split up again.'

'He was to say that he had seen both our dead bodies if he was captured.'

'We fell in with another group of German soldiers.'

'Rogues and opportunists.'

'But they helped us bribe our way through the Russian lines.'

'We slept in ruins amongst garbage and corpses.'

'We made our way on at night.'

'We took rations from dead soldiers.'

'We made our way to the Allied lines eventually.'

'And we surrendered as civilians.'

'We were never civilians. We surrendered as German soldiers.'

'I'm certain we changed into civilian clothes.'

'No. We wore military uniforms.'

'The Americans interrogated us.'

'It was the British.'

'We told them we were refugees.'

'We told them we were conscripts from Austria.'

'We told them elaborate stories about our hardships and loss.'

'We told them nothing.'

'There were other senior Nazis all throughout the detention camp, all dressed as civilians.'

'We were the only ones who made it out alive.'

'And we heard the stories of how the Russians had taken the bunker and found your charred body.'

'We heard stories that I had escaped.'

'They said Hitler was definitely dead.'

'They said Hitler was definitely alive.'

The two men look at each other and suddenly there is an enormous explosion above their head.

'The car bomb!' says Bormann.

'Yes,' agrees Hitler. 'The car bomb.'

Uncle didn't wait for me! I ran up the road, being careful not to take too large steps, and saw the fire shooting out of the sprinkler. It would have looked better at night, of course. And one of the statues had exploded. Uncle said I could help fire them off! Or he said perhaps. Always perhapses!

I walk along the street from the other side of the road to try and see what else has happened. I can see Mr Wright telling men what to do. He's telling one man to go and open the front door, but the man doesn't want to do it. Mr Wright is angry with him and is ordering him, but still the man won't do it. He tells another man to go around to the back door, but he won't go either. Mr Wright is losing his temper now, and all the men are shouting at each other. The men are telling him that if he wants somebody to go into the house it should be him, but I can see that he doesn't want to do it either.

Finally one of the men goes up the stairs with a hammer in his hand and smashes in the glass of the door on the balcony. He goes into the house and comes out again soon, saying there is nobody at home. Uncle and his friend will be in the bunker by now. They'll be safe there. But they won't be able to fire any more of their secret weapons.

I cross over the road and stand behind the council vans. The men are all still running around like they've never seen a secret weapon in their lives, trying to figure out how to turn off the flames from the sprinkler. Mr Wright and some of the other men now go into the house. Mr Wright has a clipboard so everyone knows he's in charge. They walk through the house a few times and then go out into the backyard. One of the men points towards Uncle's shed, then they all go through the same thing again, with Mr Wright telling some of the men that they have to go and open the shed door, and the men saying that if he wants to look in the shed then he ought to be the one who goes in first.

Soon all the men are in the yard arguing all over again and it is easy to sneak into the house through the side door. Then I go to the fuse box and put a chair underneath it. I open the box and then climb down and peep out the back door. Mr Wright has lost his temper with everyone and he strides across to the shed to open the door.

I don't think he'll find Uncle in his bunker straight away. But he'll find some of our secret weapons. And he'll find all the traps I've been putting around the town to catch dogs in. And he'll find the car bomb that I built for Uncle, telling him how we could build them all over the country. Explaining to him that we needed a new way to fight wars other than by having armies so it didn't matter if the numbers weren't in your favour. If you put just a few potato masher bungers in places people weren't expecting it, you could terrorise all the bullies.

If Mr Wright finds the car bomb maybe he will know how to disarm it. So I hurry back to the fuse box where the switch for it is, taking careful steps so that I arrive exactly on a prime number.

Vierzehn

Those who want to live, let them fight, and those who do not want to fight in this world of eternal struggle do not deserve to live.

— Mein Kampf

The two old Nazis open the door from the bunker cautiously. It takes them some moments to make out clearly what has happened. There is dust and smoke all about them. The workbench above their heads is covered in metal sheets, and debris lies all about. They can hear shouting men outside. There is a fire near the front of the shed. The car bomb has predominantly exploded upwards, through the windows and canvas sunroof of the Volkswagen. The resultant explosion has lifted the roof off the shed and the back walls appear to have collapsed inwards.

Bormann refrains from commenting how the shed no longer overlaps the neighbour's property.

'What do we do now?' he asks.

'We prime the death ray,' says Hitler. 'They will be distracted for some time, but we must be prepared for our break-out.'

They close the door in the workbench and make their way back down into the bunker. Blondi looks up at them expectantly, and then lays her head back down on her paws.

'Take this cord and plug it into the wall socket,' says Hitler.

Bormann does as he is instructed.

'Now,' says Hitler. 'Let me see if I can remember how to prime this. We can test it down here to make sure it will be operating effectively. We can use one of the tins of food as a target. The contents should boil and then the tin should explode when the ray is focused on it.'

'*Jawohl*,' says Bormann and sets up a tin of baked beans, and then holds the small satellite dish pointing towards it.

'Now,' says the Führer, 'First we turn on this. And then this. And now, we are ready.'

Bormann nods, holding the satellite dish like a gun.

'Then we fire,' says Hitler and turns a final knob.

Bormann looks expectantly at the tin of baked beans. He licks his lips as the death ray starts to hum and crackle. 'It is working,' he says and he keeps his eyes fixed on the tin of baked beans.

The crackle and static then becomes the sound of a television news commentator, saying, '…just confirming that breaking story – the Argentinian forces on the Falklands have surrendered to the British in what Mrs Thatcher is calling a great victory.'

Hitler and Bormann look at each other and all the strength seems to go out of Hitler. He takes a few steps backwards and sits down in one of the chairs. Bormann looks at him and looks at the tin of baked beans and then he lowers the satellite dish. The news commentator continues talking of the white flags over Port Stanley and the British troops reportedly walking freely on the streets. Then the death ray hisses and sizzles and some vital component pops with a flash. Then it is quiet.

Bormann smells the acrid smoke smell of burnt-out parts and tries to say something appropriate. But what is there to say? The Führer sighs and his body slumps like that of an old, old man. Bormann would rather he rant and throw himself on the carpet than this. He kneels down beside him and says, 'The scientists have betrayed you. Like all their empty promises of the atomic bomb. Saving the technology to sell to the Allies.'

But it has no effect. The Führer sighs again and says, 'It is all over, isn't it?'

This is the way he was in the Berlin bunker. Filled with a heavy defeatist torpor. It had taken all of Bormann's energies to shake him out of it. But he was a much younger man then and he doubts he has the energies to do it again. He feels like an old, old man himself. He drags the other chair over and slumps into it, mirroring his leader.

After some time, Hitler looks up at him and says, 'Tell me the truth, Bormann. Has Doctor Mengele developed the genetic cure for ageing?'

And Bormann, despite himself, tells the truth. 'No, *mein Führer*,' he says. 'He has not. 'In fact…' but he cannot go on. Not until Hitler orders him.

'Tell me, Bormann, what have you been trying to tell me for so long?'

Bormann tires to hold his tongue in his head, but the words force their way out, breaking out into the bunker's dusty air. 'Mengele is dead.'

Hitler stares at him for some time and then says, 'Tell me how he died.'

And Bormann lets the story free. 'Mengele went from hideout to hideout, each a little more decrepit than the one before it. He lived in Argentina, then Paraguay and then in Brazil, where he managed a farm under the alias Peter Hochbichler. He was a guest of many Nazi sympathisers but became a very lonely and depressed old man, spending long hours either working on his memoirs, perpetually trying to retell history as he believed it should be told, or writing long letters to his relatives in Germany, that were rarely answered.'

Hitler says nothing.

'As his protectors died, he was passed around to any supporters that could be found, until he came to be living with a Hungarian family on a farm in Brazil. They believed he was a minor Nazi official, but the hunt for Mengele was gaining publicity around the world, and when they found out his true identity they insisted he leave them. He then lived in a small apartment in São Paulo, going under the name of Wolfgang Gerhard. And, like so many old Nazis, he was perpetually looking out for Israeli agents in the dark corners. He was a nervous figure, chewing his moustache incessantly, and it led to fur balls building up in his intestines, causing him bowel troubles.'

Hitler nods, like he is not surprised to hear this.

'By 1978, when I last saw him, he was a sick man, fixated only on mending bridges with his son Rolf, who had rejected him.'

'And his death?' Hitler asks.

'He died in 1979. He went to visit some friends' beach cottage and he had a stroke while swimming in the sea. He is buried in a decrepit graveyard, next to a Chinaman, I recall.'

Hitler says nothing for a long, long time and then Bormann adds, 'I always thought it odd that sightings of Mengele increased most in the years after his death.'

Then Bormann too falls silent. Blondi farts.

And then Hitler says, 'So here we are again, at the end of everything, in the bunker.'

And Bormann closes his eyes. He is back in the bunker dream. He knows that the Führer is going to reach into his pocket and pull out the cyanide capsules. He will tell him that he should have left him to die in Berlin rather than let him come to this. And he will ask him to destroy his body. To be the one left behind who has to do this. But Bormann has come to understand that life without the Führer will not be a life worth living. He is who he is solely because of the Führer!

But what Hitler says is, 'So, we must plan for our break-out!'

Bormann opens his eyes.

Hitler is sitting up in his chair and his eyes have that gleam in them. 'National socialism must not be allowed to die in a small town at the end of the world. It is up to us to ensure it lives on!'

'*Jawohl, mein Führer!*' says Bormann and struggles up to his feet and gives his leader the Nazi salute.

'Sit down, sit down,' says Hitler. 'We must plan for the future.' Then he himself stands up and walks over to the trestle table. He pushes all the maps aside. 'We have been fools,' he says. 'We have been looking to the past, not the future.' He turns and looks at Bormann. 'There is a new way of waging war in the world,' he says. 'But we have been too slow to acknowledge it. It is as new as Blitzkrieg was in the

1920s and 1930s. It is no longer about having the most superior army. It is about sowing the most terror. You can do this with an army of ten or less. Don't dress in uniforms and march against your enemy, do you see? Dress like them and infiltrate into their society.'

Bormann nods slowly, not quite understanding.

'We failed in 1945 because the weight of the collapsing army weighed me down with them. We must do this without an army.'

'How?' asks Bormann.

'The Palestinians have showed us the way,' Hitler says. 'A small band of fanatics held the world to ransom during the Munich Olympics ten years ago. And they showed us how they can kill Jews.'

Now Bormann starts to understand.

'Do you know what the young German terrorist groups call themselves?' he asks Bormann. 'The children of Hitler!' He thumps his fist into his palm. Then he says, 'You win Uno when you only have one card in your hand, not many.'

Bormann is less sure he understands that reference.

'If some ragtag Arabs can achieve so much with car bombs,' says Hitler, 'think what two aged Nazis might do!'

And Bormann says, 'It is pure genius.' The determined genius of evil to survive.

'Massed armies will not be able to stand against us,' says the Führer, pointing a finger into the air. 'A new Reich is born tonight. A fourth Reich. Terror will reign until National Socialism is adopted once more – by any name.'

And Bormann is infected with Hitler's vision. As he always was. As he always needed to be. He is almost so overcome with emotion at this moment that he could throw himself into his Führer's arms and hug him. Fortunately his aged knees prevent him from such a spontaneous show of emotion and he maintains the momentous dignity befitting the occasion.

Uncle and his friend will be leaving the bunker soon and will creep away. He's told me this story before, but I didn't realise it was about how he would leave Eden. But he's only got one card left in his hand now. Uno. In code that is 21 14 15. Or, if you add all the numbers together, it is 14, which added together is 5 – which is the letter E, which stands for Exiting Eden.

Most things make sense eventually if you do the sums enough.

I hope Uncle will be all right without me. He's taught me a lot, but he needs somebody to help him. Somebody as clever as me. I know what I will do when he's gone, though. I've planned this all out like a battle plan on a map. First I will find another friend. One who is lonely and angry, and I'll help him get even with all the people he needs to get even with. Like balancing out the numbers in a sum. Then I will show him how he can be more powerful by getting a job on the local council. Mr Wright's job will be empty now that he's dead. Then from the local council he can go into politics. It is an easy step when you know what to do, as Uncle explained to me.

I will tell him that if you really want to have power you need to help people to hate somebody. Migrants or refugees or Aborigines – it doesn't matter who. If you let people hate somebody else, you become their leader. And if you can get them to hate and fear something or somebody enough, you can even become leader of the whole country. I will find a new friend who wants to have that much power and I'll tell him how to achieve it.

But I'll never tell him the biggest secret of all. The one that Uncle never understood. That if people turn against you they can take all your power away from you. Except if you are unseen and unknown. Then you just need to find another friend and start over again. No perhapses.

Fünfzehn

For there is one thing we must never forget…
the majority can never replace the man.

– Mein Kampf

It is well after dark when the two old men make their way up out of the bunker. They can see by the streetlights that there are police cars parked out the front of the house and they can see one of the council cars still in the driveway, its windscreen shattered. They wait a while and see a lone policeman walking back and forward with a torch in his hand.

'Come,' says Hitler softly, and the two men start picking their way through the debris.

The clearest path is towards the back of the shed. They hear the policeman talking on his radio and they crouch low. Hitler pressing his hand to Blondi's muzzle to make sure she doesn't growl. It takes them some time to quietly work their way clear of the remains of the shed until they are in the darkest corner of the backyard.

'Where now?' asks Bormann.

'We advance through Poland,' says Hitler and he leads Bormann to Mr Dikowski's fence.

There are large sections that have been knocked out and it is easy for the two old warriors to climb through it.

They make their way around to the front of the house and see that the front rooms are brightly lit. There are several trucks parked in the driveway.

'Television crews,' says Bormann.

Inside the house they can see Mr Dikowski giving an interview.

The bright lights illuminate him like an animal in a spotlight, thinks Bormann.

'I would prefer a German car,' says Hitler, pointing to Mr Dikowski's old white Nissan van, 'but considering the circumstances, a vehicle made by our Japanese allies will have to do. Can you start this without a key?' he asks Bormann,

'Does the Pope defecate in the woods?' asks Bormann.

'Excellent,' says Hitler.

Ten minutes later, the two old Nazis see the lights of Eden fade behind them for the last time. It is going to be a long drive to Queensland, they know, but they are full of new-found optimism.

'This premier, Mr Bjelke-Petersen,' Hitler says. 'He is going to need two advisors who understand the importance of history, to convince him to run for the office of prime minister of this country.'

And Bormann says, 'A brilliant strategy, *mein Führer*. Brilliant! But we need to stop soon so I can pee.'